HAVEN 3
by Misty Vixen

D1708178

CHAPTER ONE

David walked into the abandoned campgrounds that were now his home, passing slowly through the main gate.

He took a deep breath, held the chilled air in his lungs, and let it out slowly in a puff of haze.

He felt good.

Despite everything, despite the cold and the somewhat precarious situation they found themselves in and the potential threat of attack day and night...he felt good. Elated, actually. He continued his slow walk in between the initial few structures, which still remained abandoned.

Two weeks. It had been two weeks since that day that the thieves had made their assault on his home, and had successfully been repelled.

For the time being at least.

He felt like that moment had been a good call to arms and it was then he had made up his mind to go after them.

Unfortunately, the world had different plans.

That night, a bad storm had begun, and it hadn't let up for three solid days. They'd all pretty much been stuck in their cabins, snowed in, waiting for the worst of it to pass. It let up on the fourth day, but then barely twenty four hours had gone by before another blizzard descended on them. And so it had gone for two whole weeks.

Even during the lulls in the storms, when they had the opportunity to leave, all of their time was taken up by tasks necessary to stay alive.

Chopping firewood. Melting snow for water. Hunting game for food. Making crucial repairs to the inhabited buildings to keep the cold out and the warmth in.

Even when he managed to get away from the campgrounds, it was only to hunt the surrounding buildings for supplies. They were having to go farther and farther out at this point. He usually went with either Cait, Ellie, or Ashley.

Surprisingly, Ellie had stuck around for most of the two weeks. Although she'd disappeared about four days ago and had yet to return.

He thought she'd gotten cabin fever, or maybe she was just sick of them.

David walked up to the first of the places he intended to visit this morning. He had just finished taking a little stroll around the exterior of the campgrounds, making sure nothing was out there, nothing lurking.

Besides a few zombies stumbling around off in the distance, he didn't see anything. He stepped up to one of the cabins and knocked on the door.

A moment later it opened up and the old man who had initially been living with Ashley and her family answered. David had come to know him as Paul. He, his wife, and the young child they had essentially adopted and were now caring for had taken up residence in one of the cabins. Paul smiled as soon as he saw him.

"David," he said.

"Hello, Mister Walsh. How are you doing today?" David replied.

"Fine, David. And I believe I asked you to call me Paul, and you agreed to that. I've already got enough reminders of how old I am."

David chuckled. "Sorry, habit of mine. Do you need anything, Paul?"

"Yes, actually. We're running low on firewood. I went to get some at sunrise, but the bin's empty. I would've chopped some, but you and Evelyn advised us not to go out unless we absolutely had to...not that I'm necessarily complaining. I've had enough outdoors and winter to last me for the rest of my life, all six months of it," he replied, laughing softly.

That was another thing he was getting used to: Paul's dark sense of humor. Hell, not just his but his wife's and the other older woman who had since moved in.

They were always joking about death.

He supposed it was one way to deal with it.

"I'll make sure you get some firewood. Anything else?" David asked, pulling out the notebook he'd found and started carrying around for this.

Doing morning rounds had become part of his routine at this point.

"No, we're good otherwise. Thank you for checking in, and, uh, thank you again for taking us all in. It's very, *very* appreciated. And if there's anything either myself or Martha can do to help out, please don't hesitate to tell us. I admit it's been nice getting my breath back after all the madness, but before long it's going to feel strange, not pulling my own weight."

"You could consider this retirement," David replied, replacing the notebook after making the notation.

Paul snorted ruefully. "Son, we don't get to retire anymore. Retirement is a long dirt nap, nowadays."

"I guess so," David murmured. "When I think of something, I'll let you know, I promise."

Because he could understand that. It'd feel weird, living with other people and not doing anything in return. In a world where it felt like everyone always needed to pitch in, where it seemed like there was often more work than workers, the need to get shit done was powerful.

Especially if you felt like you were sitting on your ass at the expense of other people. But for now the place was running pretty smoothly.

Although he did intend to get more organized, and soon, he just...kept getting distracted. Living in close proximity to five women who were all highly sexual and highly interested in you tended to be very...exhausting.

On top of dating Evelyn, April, and Cait, Ellie usually jumped him once a day or so, and Ashley had revealed herself to be downright amorous. She was one horny fucking woman, and she seemed to have taken a particular liking to him. And to Ellie. And interestingly, it seemed like Ellie was returning that interest.

More than once they'd gone off on their own. And he'd had to hear about it from her parents more than once.

David stepped up to the next cabin and knocked. This time, Jim Carlson, the man who he had helped at the abandoned gas station a few weeks ago, answered.

"Hello, David," he said.

"Hello, Jim," David replied, remembering that Jim had told him something similar about what to call him. "How's everything going this morning?"

"Good, for the most part. We need more food, though." He looked a little embarrassed. "I thought I'd been doing a decent job taking care of it, but two kids, one of them being a damned teenager...they can *eat*."

"Yeah I remember what it was like," David

murmured.

"Amanda's on guard duty now and I intended to go hunting."

David considered his words. It was interesting. It wasn't exactly a question, but it wasn't exactly a statement, either. At this point, he and Evelyn and now Cait, too, were sort of seen as leaders of the community.

People weren't coming to them for everything, but...they asked a lot of questions. They all clearly wanted to be part of a community, and all that went with that.

"I haven't seen anything around but some zombies in the distance," David replied finally. "I guess, let Amanda know when you leave and where you're going, and it'd be great if you didn't go *too* far. We haven't seen those assholes for two weeks, but...they know where we are."

"Yeah," Jim muttered. "I hear you."

"All right. Good luck on hunting. I'll make sure to bring some food over today."

"Thanks."

David glanced at the main building as he began crossing to the next cabin to check on their only new arrivals since they'd invited Ashley's group and Jim's group to live with them. He was starving, and on the way out, he'd smelled bacon frying up in the kitchen. He figured Evelyn was making breakfast.

He wanted to eat. But no breakfast yet. He walked over to the next cabin and knocked on the door.

Ann was a pretty hardcore older woman. Although she was, he guessed, in her sixties, she had not only been taking care of three kids by herself since the village fell, but managed to make it to them during a blizzard about a week ago.

The place they had been staying at had been attacked by a small horde of zombies and the resulting battle, which she had been winning, had caused a fire, forcing them to abandon the property.

She already knew about their little setup here, and so she'd led the children off through the snowstorm, and had actually made it there. She was still pretty fit and capable, and had proven it since showing up.

Although she spent a lot of her time tending to the three children she'd basically adopted, she also had no problem pulling guard duty, helping when the occasional zombie or other mutated monster showed up, chopping firewood, or making repairs around the place. She was definitely extremely helpful.

She answered her door promptly and looked a little worried. "Oh, David, good. I just wanted to let you know that one of the kids is sick. I don't think it's anything serious, just a cough and a fever right now, but I'm going to go get some medicine."

"All right. Let me know if they get any worse."

"I will," she said.

"Do you need anything else today?"

"No, we're fine for other supplies. Thank you."

She headed off for the main structure, where they kept their stores of supplies: food, clean water, medicine, weapons. He looked at the cabin across from him, the one nearest to the main office on the right side, where Ashley and her family lived. He always felt uncomfortable talking with either of her parents.

Although, to his knowledge, they didn't *know* he was banging the fuck out of their daughter on a regular basis, he felt they probably suspected heavily.

It had to be awkward. He also wasn't sure how they felt about his current relationship status. Living around inhumans was one thing, dating more than one of them was quite another.

Although it might not be very obvious to the casual observer that he and April were dating, given her shyness, it was certainly common knowledge that he and Cait and Evelyn were dating.

They both had no problem kissing him on the mouth frequently and visibly.

Not that he had a problem with it.

Ashley was at least attempting to be discreet, though he wasn't entirely sure why. Either she was embarrassed to be seen with him because it would make her parents uncomfortable, or because it would make her uncomfortable, or because he was so obviously in a relationship with at least two other women, or something else entirely. But she'd been a little more...careless, lately.

Especially with Cait.

They kissed a lot, too, and not always behind what might be considered closed doors. Not that he minded that, either.

Speaking of which, the front door to Ashley's family's cabin opened up as he approached and the woman herself came out.

"Hey you," she said brightly as they came to stand together.

"Hey, Ash, how are you doing? I was just coming to see if you or your family needs anything," David replied.

"Aren't you sweet? No, we're fine. I just got done checking that myself. I intended to ask Ellie or Cait if they wanted to go out and do some hunting or exploration today," she said.

"Cait just got off nightwatch," David replied. They began walking towards the main office.

"Oh, right. Well, just Ellie, then...fuck, she isn't here, is she? I just remembered. She didn't show up at any time last night, did she?"

"I..." he hesitated, thinking about it. "I don't think so. But you know her, she can sneak in and out with a little too much ease."

"Yeah, I guess so."

As they walked in and headed upstairs into the kitchen and dining area, David laughed softly. A certain blue-furred jag was sitting at the table. He could tell immediately that Ellie was agitated, between the look on her face and the way her tail twitched back and forth.

Across the hall, through the open window that looked into it, David spied Ann talking with Evelyn, who was finishing up making breakfast.

"Ellie! I'm so glad you're here," Ashley said.

Ellie smiled warmly and it seemed to break through her agitation and unease for a moment. "Hello, Ashley. I missed you, too."

"I was just going to ask if we could go on another excursion today."

She opened her mouth to respond, then hesitated and her smile faded. "I'm afraid not. I'm sorry." She looked squarely at David. "You and I need to talk. Alone."

He felt a chill splash his guts. "What's wrong?" he asked.

"Nothing immediately dangerous, just...a serious talk we need to have. Have you had breakfast yet?" she asked.

"No, not yet."

"Okay. We'll eat, and then we can take a walk."

"...all right," David replied. He was tempted to try and get it out of her here and now, but immediately shot that idea down.

No way he was getting Ellie to tell him even a single thing before she was good and ready to. Well great, now he had that responsibility dumped in his lap. Hopefully it wasn't *too* serious, whatever it was...what could it be?

He had the idea that it had something to do with their...relationship?

Did they *have* a relationship?

Ellie was strange. She had no problem having sex, but also clearly kept him, and everyone else except for Cait and perhaps now Ashley, at arm's length. He respected her desires and privacy, but...

It *was* getting kind of frustrating.

But he had his own problems. Like being in a four-way relationship in a post-apocalyptic landscape while trying to maintain a quartet of families attempting to form a community. Too often, he felt like he simply didn't have time for everyone. Speaking of which...

"Where's April?"

"Still in bed," Evelyn called. "With Cait."

"Oh. Okay then," David said. "I'm going to go...check on them."

"Don't get distracted," Ellie said, and her tone indicated that she was serious about getting a move on.

He just sighed and nodded. He'd had wake-up sex with Evelyn, but he was still horny. He jogged upstairs and listened closely as he made his way down the hallway, towards April's bedroom. He didn't hear anything, although as he drew very close to her door, which was almost closed, he heard quiet conversation.

Things had been going well with April, he thought. She was very kind to him, and clearly liked him a lot, though she still seemed very awkward. Which he understood. He'd taken the time over the past few weeks to build her a bookshelf out of scrap lumber laying around, and thought he'd done a pretty good job putting it together, even managing to sand it down.

He'd also managed to find and give her close to a dozen books so far. He had to admit, she had certainly incentivized him to do so, thanking him vigorously in her own way each time he brought one. It always resulted in a wonderfully intense orgasm for both of them.

He knocked on the door.

"Come in," Cait called sleepily.

He opened the door and stepped in. "Hello, David," she said, and yawned.

"Hi," April said, smiling tiredly.

"How are you doing today?" he asked. April had been prone to bouts of weakness and exhaustion over the past few days. She'd explained it was a combination of her anemia and insomnia, and her tendency to get too involved in her projects to remember to eat properly.

"I definitely need more sleep today," she replied. She giggled. "Especially after what Cait just did to me."

"I'm sorry I missed it," he replied.

"Me too, but...I've still got enough energy to perform again, you know," Cait said, smirking tiredly at him.

He groaned. "It is...*so* fucking tempting, it truly is, but Ellie has demanded my presence and warned me not to dawdle."

"Oh, she's back?" Cait asked. "I must've missed her on my way in."

"I think she just got here."

"Well, I know how she gets when she's in one of her moods. Don't let us keep you. Come wake me up for a bang when you're free though. You know I'm always ready for you, handsome," she said.

She looked beyond sexy right now, the blankets almost, but not quite, covering up her large, bare breasts, her face slicked with sweat, her red hair a wild mess as she laid beside an equally nude April, who had a very satisfied look on her face.

"I promise I will," he replied. "Have a good sleep, my lovers."

"Be dreaming of you, I'm sure, David," Cait said.

It was hard, but he left them, closing the door behind him and heading back downstairs. *Damn* did he want to fuck right now! Cait was an *exceptional* lover. Not that he didn't appreciate Evelyn or April. Although if Ellie was pulling him off somewhere, he'd absolutely love to be inside of her. He wouldn't say it out loud but...

She had the best pussy, so far.

Good fucking God did she have such an amazing vagina. And she could *fuck*. Oh could that woman fuck so good.

An uncomfortably powerful erection accompanied him by the time he headed into the kitchen. Ann had since left, and now Evelyn was finishing up the meal. He could hear Ellie and Ashley chatting in the dining room.

"Hey, honey. I assume all's well out there?" Evelyn asked.

"Yeah, although Jim's family needs more food, and Paul's almost out of firewood, and we *are* out of firewood. Jim's going hunting, too," he reported.

Evelyn sighed. "I guess it's for the best. I intend to deal with the firewood problem today. It's what I'm going to do for the next several hours, in fact. Ellie popped in before sitting at the table. We had a conversation. She's going to have a similar conversation with you when you go out for a walk with her."

"What does she want to talk about? I'm nervous," David asked.

"She asked me not to tell you. It's...important, I'll say that. She wants to put it in her own words. Just listen to her, talk with her. She's smart and she knows what she's talking about. It involves all of us here. Now, help me carry this food in."

"All right," he replied after a few seconds. He really wanted to know more, but he'd just have to wait. Evelyn leaned down and gave him a kiss, and then they began gathering up the food she'd prepared. It was mostly bacon and scrambled eggs and hashbrowns, all of it gotten from the farm. Their deal had worked out nicely so far. He thought about his relationship with Evelyn as they set the table for breakfast.

She was...patient. Which was good, given how busy they both were. He thought it helped that it was her bed that he came to almost every night. They'd finished their project last week, building a custom-made bed frame big enough for her and him, (and one or two others), and then they'd spent a few hours breaking it in.

He was glad they hadn't literally broken it, because they had gone pretty rough. Especially when

Cait and Ellie had jumped in at one point. And April. And then Ashley, later on. Such a fuck that had been.

They were getting along well, and mainly she seemed to want to just be around him. It didn't really matter what they were doing, so long as it was together. Consequently, he found himself happily patrolling outside, chopping firewood, making repairs to the cabins, or taking long walks to check out abandoned buildings in her company.

Sometimes they had long, pleasant conversations. Sometimes they walked in lengthy bouts of companionable silence. That sense of intimacy, of connection, had only strengthened over the past few weeks.

He and Evelyn set the table, and the four of them began to dish out food for themselves. Feeling the press of time and knowing that he had a lot of walking ahead of him, David didn't go too heavy on the food. That, and he was actually pretty eager to get going. It had been several days since his last real excursion beyond the fences that surrounded the campgrounds, and surprisingly, he was itching to go out.

Plus, he *really* wanted to know what was so important that Ellie *had* to tell him, herself, alone. He wasn't sure whether to be excited or nervous, though from what Evelyn had said, he didn't think it was anything to get excited for. Like sex.

They all considered sex important, sure, but probably not in the context she had placed it in. Or maybe he was totally off base and it was something sexual? Maybe she wanted to be in a relationship with him?

He was even less sure about that one. It seemed more unlikely. This was the problem with having *no* fucking information. David just made himself relax, eat, and be patient.

He'd find out soon enough.

"So what are you guys actually like *doing* out there that I can't come too?" Ashley asked eventually.

"David and I have something important to discuss," Ellie replied.

"Oh really? Is it serious? Are *you two* serious now? Boyfriend and girlfriend?" Ashley asked, smirking.

"No," Ellie replied simply. Well, that answered that. Unless she just didn't want to admit it to Ashley.

"Yeah, I guess he's got enough of those, huh?" she asked, still with that smirk.

David sighed. Ashley had a habit of teasing him a lot. He glanced at Evelyn. She winked at him and then turned to Ashley. "Is that your not-so-subtle way of saying you're interested in taking things to the next level with David?"

"What?" she asked, startled, immediately losing her smirk. "No. That's not-no. I'm happy with the way things are."

Both Evie and Ellie laughed.

"Not so fun to be on the other end, huh?" David asked.

She sighed heavily. "Whatever. Just don't take too long fucking out there in the woods. I want another expedition today."

"I'll see what I can do," Ellie replied, and finished off her meal. She began to say something else and then her gaze jerked to the side, her eyes widening. "There's a mouse," she said.

David looked over and saw a little white mouse scurrying across the floor. "Oh, hey! There you are," he said, and plucked a piece of bacon off his plate.

He tossed it onto the floor in the mouse's path. The mouse hesitated and put its little nose up in the air. It twitched a few times, then it regarded them cautiously for a few seconds, then it began scurrying over to the bacon.

"You know this mouse?" Ellie asked.

"Yes. This is Frostbite. He lives here," Evelyn replied.

"He showed up last week. Caught him in the pantry, trying to get into our food. Luckily, we're adamant about sealing it up, so he didn't get in, but we feed him now," David said.

"He's smart. And brave. He's learned to come ask for food during mealtimes, usually when I'm preparing. I guess he was outside while I was cooking today," Evelyn murmured.

"So you've got a pet now?" Ellie asked.

"Yeah, I guess you could say that. He lives here and we named him and we feed him. Although he seems pretty independent," David replied.

"Huh. Well, okay then."

She sat back and crossed her arms, waiting impatiently for David to finish. So he did, tossing what was left of his meal into his mouth. He kissed Evelyn and then when she complained, went for a kiss with Ashley as well. She grabbed his shirtfront and pulled him into a hard, long kiss on the mouth.

Before she fully released him, she looked up at him and said, "We haven't fucked for two days, David. You'd better fix that soon."

"Uh...yeah, I can do that," he replied.

She laughed and released him. "Good."

Ellie was already on her feet. "We should go."

"All right, let me get my gear," David replied, and hurried upstairs.

CHAPTER TWO

"Okay," David said as they struck out away from the campgrounds, "mind telling me what the big secret is now?"

He'd grabbed his gear, which wasn't too time-consuming, given he'd already been wearing his cold-weather clothes and had his pistol on him. Really, he'd just needed to snag his backpack, which he made sure to pre-load whenever he was finished with it.

He always ensured there was a small supply of emergency medical supplies, food, water, and a change of clothes tucked away in the bottom. He'd also grabbed four spare magazines of ammo. He'd been half-tempted to snag the submachine gun he had hidden away in their makeshift armory, but ultimately figured it'd do better at home, just in case anything happened while he was away.

"We need to talk about your plans for the future," Ellie replied after a moment, as though she had been considering how to word it.

"I mean...okay? Why? Is there something specific you want to talk about?"

Ellie sighed after another few seconds. "David, you and Evelyn, and now Cait, to a certain degree, are responsible for people now. I don't question your motives. By now, I feel fairly confident that I know you and Evelyn, and that the things you do...you do to help, and for no other reason. And that's good. That's great. It's very rare, and it should be cherished, when people do things like that," she said.

He noticed she wasn't looking at him as they walked on, and her tail was twitching intensely. "So what's the other shoe to this, then?" he asked.

"I'm worried that you don't appreciate the severity of the task you have decided to tackle, nor the reality of your situation," she replied, her voice growing firm.

David felt an instinctual response in him, one leaping to his own defense, that he goddamned well knew what he was doing, as did Evelyn, but he kept his mouth shut and waited for that initial fire to pass. Ellie wouldn't be saying this to his face without a good reason.

During their time together, he'd learned that she was blunt, but not cruel, and rarely was she flat out wrong. He thought he had a decent handle on things at the campground, but sometimes he wondered, and he *did* know he could be doing more.

"Okay," he said eventually, "elaborate."

Ellie seemed relieved. "You've been doing a good job so far, watching out for people, setting a watch, maintaining the basic supplies, working out a deal with the farmers. It's good. You've been doing great."

He felt a flash of irritation. "I don't need my ego stroked, Ellie."

"That isn't what I'm doing," she replied firmly, looking over at him now, staring hard into his eyes.

Now he felt a flash of remorse. "Sorry," he murmured.

"It's fine. This isn't the most fun conversation. I just wanted to let you know that you're on the right path. You have the right idea. You and Evie both. But I think you aren't looking far enough into the future, nor are you steeling yourselves enough.

"When something happens like what happened at River View, I think people typically have one of two responses. They're terrified it's going to happen again, or they tell themselves they got through the worst of it and relax. And unfortunately, in the world we live in now, that first response is the healthier one. It pays to be paranoid."

"So we're not being paranoid enough?" he asked.

"I think so. Not to mention the fact that more people are going to come, David. A safe place that isn't run by a fucking asshole and you don't have to make huge sacrifices for? That's *so* rare. People will want to live there with you. Too many, probably. There's a lot of people scattered across the region, and more could arrive at any moment, given how many people are mobile nowadays. And you would be downright shocked at how fast food goes. Even for the amount of people you have right now. I think you need to be more desperate."

"Desperate?"

"Yes. You need to be treating your situation more desperately. I think you're distracted by all the pussy you're getting, and that you don't fully appreciate what it means to run a village, and *yes,* I acknowledge that I'm contributing to the distraction. It's just...I like you. That's why I'm telling you all this. For your sake, but also because I *am* a fan of helping people, and I know that you really do want what's best for everyone."

"I like you too, and...this *is* appreciated," David murmured.

"Good, I'm glad. And that's not even the worst part."

"What *is* the worst part?" he asked cautiously.

"You have the right idea, going after those thieving assholes, but they aren't the only ones we'll have to worry about. I mean, there's always the threat of more like them showing up, trying to shake us down, or just kill us and take what we've got. I'm always paranoid about Stern and his group of military assholes.

"They aren't *all* bad, but...enough of them are that I'm worried. They've got access to some serious firepower. Then there's the fact that there's so many stalkers. You remember how many nearly ripped us to shreds when we were recovering those solar panels."

"Yeah..." he whispered. He still had nightmares.

"That amount of stalkers is *unheard of,* David. I mean, they're dead now, but that still bugs me, and there's a lot of stalkers in the region. That could develop into something someday." She sighed. "And that's just what we *know* about. I think you all could afford to be more...aggressive, in your planning and preparation."

"Aggressive in what way?" he asked.

"Don't get me wrong. I am in no way suggesting you attack people. But, for example, how much water do you have stored?"

"Maybe twenty gallons," he replied.

"You could easily have five times that. You should be filling a basement with stored, purified water. This snow isn't going to last forever, and yeah, we've got a river and a lake, but we've got no idea what might happen in the future. The point is, we have snow, a *lot* of snow, right now, and we can one hundred percent for sure melt a shitload of snow and store a shitload of water. I took a peek at your food supply, nowhere near enough. And your firewood is depleted. It should never be depleted. And there's still holes in your fences."

He sighed heavily. "I know, I know."

"These are just examples."

"So what should I do, then?" he asked. "Go after the thieves now or start hardcore stocking up on shit?"

"Thieves first," she replied immediately. "If you have something actively threatening you while you're trying to do something, you always eliminate the threat first, otherwise it just has that many more opportunities to fuck you and your shit up. But I think you should set up some kind of schedule today, get the people there more involved."

"Yeah, that's a good idea." Paul wasn't the only one getting a little antsy about not having enough to do. They were all grateful to have a safe place to lay their heads, but people usually didn't like to idle for too long.

This would be good for everyone.

"Will you help?" he asked finally.

"Yes," Ellie replied. "I will help you take down the thieves. Although I'm going to admit, I'm not as good with manual labor."

"I think eliminating those assholes will be more than sufficient, and I definitely appreciate the assistance." He frowned. "I still want to get those fuckers. Evie's leg is doing fine now, but...goddamnit. That was too close."

"Yeah, I'm with you there." She pointed. "There's the building I was talking about. We haven't been there yet, I think."

He could just make it out off in the distance, through the trees.

He and the others had been making a slowly widening circle out away from the campgrounds over the past two weeks, when they could get out. Like he and Ashley had done when they'd first had sex.

There were a number of abandoned houses,

cabins, and other structures littering the land. Though most of them were picked clean by decades of scavengers, some still held the occasional lost treasure or tucked-away cache some unknown person had hidden months or even years ago and never came back for.

They had been adding to their map, marking off structures one by one.

From what he had gathered, there weren't too many left to search. Which would put them in a tough spot, potentially. A cold wind blew and he shivered as they continued, making their way between the trees and keeping an eye out for hostiles.

So far, the zombies hanging around hadn't taken notice of them, and he'd tended not to fire his gun if he could manage it. Not only did he want to save the bullets, given how hard they were to produce nowadays, but it also paid to be quieter.

Although zombies could occasionally be their own resources, given sometimes, and it was rare but it did happen, they died with backpacks or crucial things in their pockets.

Neither spoke as they made their final approach on the building, which turned out to be a simple two-story house. Most of the windows were broken out and the back door was bashed in. The withered remnants of vines crept up across the back of the structure.

Inside, he thought he could see something moving, shuffling about. Ellie drew her combat knife, and he did the same. If it was just zombies, they could probably save ammo.

Ellie indicated she wanted to go in first as they approached the back door. He nodded and let her, given she was the more capable and experienced fighter of the two. She stepped up to the door, paused, then slipped inside.

He stepped up to the back door and watched as she moved swiftly through a little transition room with three doors. The left door was closed, but the right door was just a doorway that led into the kitchen, same with the one dead ahead, but it led into a hallway. It was dark in the hall. Ellie went into the kitchen and he stepped into the first room, knife ready.

A few seconds of silence passed, and then he heard a quiet grunt of exertion, followed by a shallow thump. Then the two noises were repeated. David began to head in after her when he heard a groan.

There was movement from ahead of him, in the darkened hallway. He waited as footsteps started coming his way, and then a zombie appeared in the daylight streaming in from behind him. It was a badly decayed man in ripped, bloodied traveling clothes that were barely hanging on him anymore.

His flesh looked loose, like it, too, was barely hanging on him anymore, giving him a sickening look. His eyes were cloudy with blood and vacant. He reached for David with filthy hands and broken fingernails, coming forward and groaning.

David readied himself. He knew how to do this, he'd done it hundreds of times before, but still, each time he had to actually face one of these things, it freaked him out. Not nearly as much as it used to, but still, something about them, several somethings probably, activated the fear center of his brain with a goddamned lightning bolt.

As the zombie came up to him, within arm's length, he drove his blade forward and stabbed the decaying, rotting thing in the eye. The blade punched through, right into its brain, and killed it in an instant.

He yanked the knife back and the body dropped.

That's when he heard shuffling from behind him and another low groan. Shit, one of them must have been hanging out around the other side of the house. He stepped back, out of the doorway, right next to it, and waited. The footsteps drew closer. Something clattered deeper in the house. A shadow fell across the floor and the awful stench of rotting flesh began to fill the room. The zombie stepped inside and walked past him.

Perfect.

David drove the blade into the base of its skull, severing its brain stem and killing it instantly. He slipped the knife back out as it dropped to join its brother. As that happened, Ellie appeared in the hallway ahead of him.

"You okay?" she asked.

"Yeah," he replied.

"We're clear down here. Let's head upstairs."

David nodded and followed after her after poking his head back outside and making sure nothing else was sneaking up on him. He found it hard not to stare at her wonderfully toned ass as she walked up ahead of him.

She was right about that: he was getting distracted by sex. But it seemed impossible not to be distracted by it when he was around as many women as he was, all of whom wanted to sleep with him.

He really fucking hoped Ellie was willing to fuck during this trip.

They reached the top of the stairs. Ellie pointed to one door and then headed for another. David went towards the door she'd indicated and opened it open. It creaked in the still quiet and he winced slightly, waiting. The room beyond was lit, at least, with winter sunlight coming in through a dirty window.

A bedroom waited for him, a silent testament to whoever had once lived here, everything covered in dust. It looked undisturbed, but David took the time to do a quick hunt in any places something might be hiding.

He cleared it, and another bedroom, and a closet, and Ellie cleared the rest. After that, they headed back downstairs. David opened up the closed door by the back entrance, hoping that it didn't lead to a basement.

Thankfully, it didn't, just a closet that was almost totally barren. With the house clear, the pair began to move through it, now performing a far more thorough search for supplies. This had become such a common thing in David's life: picking through the derelict, wrecked remains of the lives of those long gone.

He always felt a vague discomfort as he shifted furniture, looked through cabinets and closets, and poked into every nook and cranny. This had been someone's life once. Maybe a couple. Maybe a family. As he often did, he found himself wondering about what life might have been like before the apocalyptic scenario that had swept his entire planet, killing billions.

There were still some people alive from those times, and they mostly told similar stories. He heard a lot about corporations. It was weird, because there really wasn't anything like that now. The closest he'd seen was groups of people who ran larger settlements with an iron fist, bleeding people dry, getting the maximum amount of work out of them while investing the most minimum amount of resources in return.

The idea that the whole world worked like that before the apocalypse made him sick to his stomach every time he thought about it.

There were so many stories. People who would go into debt for the rest of their lives when they needed a life-saving treatment. It didn't make any sense to him, what was the alternative? Die? And it wasn't as if there wasn't an abundance of resources available back then. There were a ton more people, but apparently they had far more than enough for everyone.

He still didn't fully understand why it was allowed, though he'd been told it wasn't like that *everywhere*, necessarily, mostly just in these lands he'd roamed his whole life.

Much about the world from before didn't make sense to him, and he didn't know which one was worse.

They didn't find too much in the house. The kitchen was bare, but he found a pair of books in the living room, beneath a ripped up couch. They didn't look familiar and he stashed them in his pack, glad that he could so regularly give gifts to April that made her so genuinely happy. After finding nothing else on the first floor, they headed up to the second one and split up, searching more.

One of the rooms had once belonged to a child, and he almost passed over the scattering of toys he found, but they had children of various ages living with them now. So, he began gathering up the blocks, tiny cars, and dolls he'd found.

As he was finishing up, he heard Ellie come into the room behind him. She looked at what he was packing up. "What are you doing?"

He shoved the last of it into his pack and closed

it, then turned to face her. "For the kids," he replied. "I thought it'd be nice."

"Oh..." Her confused expression softened. "That's really...kind of you." She hesitated and, strangely, looked guilty.

"What?" he asked, standing up.

"I...it's nothing," she replied, and turned away abruptly, then began walking deeper into the second story to continue her own search.

David stood still for a few seconds, wondering what *that* had been about. Did she have a problem with him taking toys? He supposed it would be in line with her personality. Ellie struck him as more of a pure survival mentality kind of woman, who might hesitate at wasting time and resources on something considered frivolous.

Well, at least she wasn't giving him shit about it, and it wasn't like he was going to change his mind. He moved on to an old bathroom and spent a little while hunting through that, searching the tub, under the sink, in the tiny built-in closet, and almost gave up.

Until he looked at the toilet tank and then lifted the lid.

"Oh fuck yes," he whispered when he saw what was inside.

Someone had stuffed a little stash in the long-dried toilet tank. He found a few magazines of nine millimeter bullets, an unmarked bottle of pills, hopefully painkillers or antibiotics, April would almost certainly be able to tell him which, and a few cans of beans.

It was obvious that it had been here a while, and hopefully whoever it was wouldn't come looking for it. David quickly took it and slipped it all into his pack, then went to join Ellie.

He found her searching the last room in the house. Her movements were stiff and he wondered if he'd pissed her off. He didn't think he'd done anything to upset her, but Ellie was...unpredictable, and kind of moody.

She didn't seem interested in talking, so he just helped her finish her search. They only found a few clothes and another book that he tucked away into his pack, then started heading downstairs.

"Did you find anything?" she asked as they headed back outside.

"Yeah. Some ammo, a bit of food and medicine," he replied.

"Oh. Good." She paused and looked around. "There's one more building I know about, a cabin. It's a little farther on, come on."

She struck off southbound again, and he followed after her.

...

"Ellie, did I piss you off?" They'd been walking for another ten minutes at this point and he couldn't take it anymore.

"What? No," she replied, looking over at him, startled.

"Then what's wrong?" he asked. She stared at him for a few seconds longer, then looked away. He sighed. "Ellie, you *can* trust me. I think I've proven that by now."

"That's not what concerns me," she murmured.

"What concerns you, then?" he asked.

"I...forming attachments concerns me," she replied. "But that's not what's bothering me.

Just...seeing you in there, with the toys, and the books you get for April, I just...it reminds me of when I was, shall we say, harsher. I wasn't always harsh, but I used to yell at people for doing things like that. For wasting time on stuff like that when survival was at stake. I certainly had a reputation for being able to keep you alive, but I didn't have any friends. I liked that. I thought attachments slowed you down."

"But...?" he asked. "I mean, obviously there's a 'but', given where you are now and what you're doing."

She sighed. "But someone eventually taught me, or really reminded me, that...a life without happiness isn't much of a life. And while it is one thing to keep myself from joy, it is much worse to do it to others. It's cruel. And I stopped doing that. But I spent what felt like a long time being like that, and seeing you and what you're doing for them, is just...it makes me feel guilty, and ashamed. I once...tossed a little girl's doll into a fire. In front of her. After ripping it from her hands."

"Fuck," David muttered, because he didn't know what else to say.

"Yeah...I thought I was helping her. I was *sure* I was helping her, in the long run. I saw myself in her, and I wished that someone had taught me to not be weak from a younger age. I thought I was saving her that pain, further down the line, when the world really came and stomped your guts out. But I wasn't. I was just being cruel, and I was wrong, and I hate it so much. I hate remembering that. I still have nightmares about it." She laughed miserably. "All the nasty, savage shit I've seen and I still have nightmares about throwing a doll into a fire and listening to a young girl cry."

"I'm so sorry," David said.

"Not as sorry as I am."

"What...happened? After?"

She sighed. "Even then, I felt guilty. I just thought it was my weakness speaking. After a few days, I finally went out looking for another doll. I found one, I gave it to her, I apologized. Her parents were mad at me, but they were also scared of me. The girl...forgave me. I don't know why. I still don't know why. I never forgave myself. In the end, the village I was at back then fell to an attack. I managed to save her and her family, and some others. I got them to another, more secure village, and then I left. I just left." She slowed down as they reached the cabin in question.

"Ellie," he said quietly, stepping up next to her, "I'm sorry."

"I don't–" she hesitated, then turned towards him. She looked more miserable than he'd ever seen her. "I don't fucking–"

He opened his arms and she immediately hugged him. He thought she would cry, and she did, a little bit, but not much. He supposed even now she had more control and was so unwilling to let herself cry. He kind of knew what it felt like.

Crying sort of felt like...a surrender. A failure. He knew that was stupid, but he couldn't help but feel that way on the occasions when he did cry.

So he stood there and held her, hugging her tightly against him, keeping an eye out for zombies. After several minutes, she let go of him and stepped back.

"I'd appreciate it if you didn't mention this to anyone," she said.

"Of course not, Ellie. I would never betray you

like that," he replied.

"Thank you," she murmured. "You're...much kinder than I deserve."

"Everyone fucks up, Ellie."

"I know. I just...that's one of those ones that's never going to leave me." She heaved a long, tired sigh. "Let's just...search this cabin and go home."

"Okay."

They checked the outside first, and once they were sure it was clear, the pair of them headed in through the front door, having to force it open. The cabin, at least, was small and simple. There were just two rooms: a bathroom and everything else. They spent half an hour picking over everything carefully, hunting beneath the furniture, in the cabinets, checking for hidden panels in the floor, the ceiling, or any of the walls.

Mostly it was a fruitless search, finding nothing but dust and trash and empty spaces, pausing occasionally to look out the windows and see if anything was creeping up on them from the outside.

But near the end, he was checking out the last corner of the main room after pulling a dresser away from the wall, and there he found it: a section of the floor was removable. It was decently well hidden, but he managed to stick his knife in the crack and popped it open without any real trouble.

Turning on the little flashlight he brought for just such occasions, he shined it down into the hole where a backpack waited. It was covered in dust and dirt and looked like it had been there for, at least, months, if not longer.

David reached in and grabbed it quickly. He was always paranoid of places like this. Anything could be down there. But no monstrous hand shot out and snagged him as he successfully retrieved the pack. Just in case, he put the section of flooring back in place and shoved the dresser back so that one of the legs of the heavy piece of furniture sat directly on the panel.

"What is it?" Ellie asked as he dropped into a crouch and unzipped the pack.

David peered in. "Cans," he said. "Vegetables, mostly," he murmured, pulling a few out and studying them. He piled up close to a dozen cans of food, each marked with simple words. Carrots, green beans, peas, corn, two cans of chopped beef. Beneath it, two bottles of water, and a combat knife, a good one, complete with a leather sheath.

"Fuck me, that's nice," he muttered, studying the blade.

He put it all back and zipped up the pack, then stood up. He realized Ellie had gone quiet and looked over at her. He half-expected her to be staring out a window, maybe having caught sight of something, but she was staring directly at him, and her gaze was steady and strong. "...what?" he asked.

A slow grin spread across her face and she stepped up to him. "You said the magic words," she replied, and she kissed him.

For a second, he had no idea what she was talking about, but he was certainly happy that this was happening. He kissed her back, hugging her to him, and she slipped her tongue easily into his mouth. He twined it with his own, enjoying her taste and the unique texture and the wonderful experience of making out with her.

When she pulled back, he said, "Oh...magic words. Fuck me."

She snorted. "David, sometimes you're kind of

thick." He felt her hand caress his crotch, where his erection strained against his clothing. "Not that that's a problem..."

"You think I've got a big dick?" he replied.

She rolled her eyes and gave him a little shove, then took off her shirt. "You're about average for length, maybe a little more," she said. "But you've definitely got girth, which is where it counts, in my book at least. Cait complains about it sometimes."

"What do you mean?" he asked. He'd never heard any complaints from Cait.

"She says sucking your dick is exhausting, she has to open her mouth as wide as possible to avoid getting her teeth on it," she replied.

"Oh." He took off his shirt. "I'm not sure how to feel about that."

"I understand," Ellie said, pulling her pants down. As usual, she had opted out of any kind of underclothes. "On the one hand, hey, big dick. On the other hand, functionally, it's causing irritation for your girlfriend. Although she's got no complaints when you stick it in her other holes, so..." she shrugged, standing nude before him now, "probably a net win."

He began to undo his pants, but she stepped up and touched his hand. "Leave them on."

"Uh, okay. Any particular reason?" he asked, unzipping his pants and beginning to work his cock out through the hole.

She shrugged. "Dunno, just like it that way. Come on. I haven't fucked in four days." She took his hand and pulled him over to the bed.

"Seriously? Who would turn you down?" he replied.

"First, I was really busy. Second, you're the only

guy I like and trust enough to let stick his cock in me at this point. I thought about swinging by the doctor's place to fuck one of them there, but, well, I was busy."

"What were you busy with?" he asked as she sat down.

"Nothing that really matters, now come *on!*" she replied, yanking him down onto the bed.

And then they were kissing again, and he was running his hands across her wonderfully fit, blue-furred body. Ellie was in fantastic shape, probably the best shape of any of the women he shared a bed with nowadays.

He groped her firm breasts, ran his hands down across her wonderful hips to her athletic thighs as she roughly kissed him. His fingertip found her clit and she let out a cry of surprised pleasure as he began to rub it.

"Oh fuck you are good with that," she whispered, eyes closed, face an inch from his as she began to revel in the pleasure of his foreplay. She shuddered against him, arching her back briefly. "You find it and touch it in just the right way immediately...oh, David, you just...oh yes..." And then she gasped and moaned loudly and kissed him again.

He grinned into the kiss and kept fingering her, pleasuring her more intensely. There was a particular, and powerful, satisfaction in pleasuring a woman like Ellie. She was so tough and confident and strong in everything she did, and she allowed him to see her at her most vulnerable, trusted him with her pleasure, with her nude body, and he was able to more than deliver, he was so happy to find.

But besides that, he just liked giving her pleasure. She deserved it. Ellie was a good person, and she'd been through so much, far more than he knew, he was learning, and a good orgasm delivered by someone you liked was one of the truest pleasures in the world, as far as David was concerned. His girlfriends seemed to agree with him.

"Oh, *David!*" she cried, and her hips bucked suddenly before he could even get a finger inside of her, and she began to come.

She was such a squirter.

"Ellie, shh!" he replied.

"I c-can't help-*oh my fucking God yes!*" she cried, and pressed a hand over her own mouth. He continued fingering her as she orgasmed, her whole body going rigid and then trembling furiously, hips jerking as she came and came and just fucking *came*. He looked up and down her wonderfully trim, fit, blue-furred body as she climaxed. She was such a sexy fucking woman. Abruptly, she stopped and reached out and grabbed him.

"Fucking get inside me *now!*" she growled.

"Okay," he replied, rolling over on top of her. She opened her legs for him, sticking them in the air as he got lined up with her.

She reached down and grabbed his cock, lined him up, and wrapped her legs around his waist, then squeezed, forcing him into her.

"Ohhhhhhhh, *Ellie...*" he groaned loudly as he slid into her.

Holy. Fucking. Shit.

He immediately began fucking her, thrusting into her, setting a furious pace right out of the gate, and she let out a long, satisfied moan of bliss as he did so. She spread her legs again, sticking them back up into the air, and laid there and let him drill the fuck out of her.

One of the absolute best things about sex with inhumans, David was forcefully reminded as he was bathed in the bliss of their sexual union, was there was no reason at all to use protection. And bareback sex was, as far as he'd been able to determine, the single greatest goddamned motherfucking pleasure in existence.

He buried his entire length into Ellie again and again, listening to her moan and cry out in impassioned ecstasy as she took his cock, pushing up with her firm, powerful hips.

And he was reminded that yes, there was no denying it: Ellie had the greatest pussy.

Barely within half a minute he was struggling not to blow his load. It just felt *too fucking good.* It was like an overload of pure pleasure, all that tight, hot, wetness. Really, it was the wetness. She was *so* fucking wet!

"Ah, yes, David! *Yes! Give me that fat fucking cock!*" she yelled, and he went harder, making the bed creak and shake violently as he pounded her fucking brains out.

Part of him knew this was really dangerous, because noise definitely attracted undead, and they were being noisy as hell, but the rest of him just could not care because the absolute rapturous gratification of plunging his cock into her as hard and as fast as he could was overwhelming him.

"This is why you didn't want me banging Cait," he growled at her.

"Yes!" she snapped, hugging him to her. "Yes, I fucking wanted this dick for myself, goddamnit! Oh God...fuck...don't stop..." she moaned.

"Gonna be tough...your pussy is just too...oh, it's *too good, Ellie...*" he groaned.

"I know-ah!-it is. Keep going...please, keep going," she begged.

It was a good thing that he'd already had sex once today, because if he hadn't, he wouldn't have been able to hold back. That, and the fact that he'd been getting a lot of practice over the past few weeks.

David held on, continuing to ram her, pushing deep down inside of her. He kissed her hard on the mouth and she moaned and kissed him back, shoving her tongue into his mouth and hugging him tightly, moving her wonderful, soft body against his own.

He knew she was trying to get another orgasm out, which he was more than happy to supply her with, but she was holding him too closely against herself for him to reach down and rub her clit, and she didn't seem at all interested in letting him go.

So he kept going, increasing the speed with which he stroked into her, fighting against the orgasm that was threatening to overwhelm and burst out of him.

"Come on, Ellie..." he moaned.

"Almost there, David! Almost...*oh holy shit David yes!*" she screamed, and he clapped his hand over her mouth.

She moaned and shrieked against it, the muffled sounds of her screams surprisingly hot, her eyes wide as she started to orgasm. He moaned loudly as he felt her vaginal muscles convulse and a huge increase in heat and wetness.

She came again, she began coming all over his dick and he immediately lost his fight with his own orgasm. And he lost it gladly. He cried out, letting out a primal grunt as he started coming inside of her.

And they orgasmed together, locked in a blissful union of total ecstasy.

He moaned and grunted, trying to keep it down as he pumped her sweet, orgasming inhuman pussy full of his seed, blowing a huge load into her. He could feel his seed leaving him in powerful spurts, each one sending a new earthquake of rapture throughout his entire body.

He came until there was nothing left in him, and then he was panting, laying against her, momentarily boneless from the exertion of the sex and the orgasm.

They laid there together for several moments, waiting for their hearts to calm down, and then he carefully pulled out of her and stood up on shaky legs.

He looked down at himself, then sighed. "*This* is why I wanted to take my pants off."

"Sorry," Ellie murmured, although she didn't sound sorry about the big wet spot all over his pants and boxers.

He just sighed again and shed his clothes. He took a moment to dig new underwear and pants out of his pack, pull them on, transfer what was in his pockets to his new pants, then stuff the stained clothes into his pack and zip it back up.

Once that was done, he pulled his shirt back on, then walked to the nearest window and looked out while Ellie began to dress. He saw a few zombies wandering around outside, very close to the cabin. They must have been drawn in by all the noise, but had lost track of them when they'd stopped.

"So we done out here?" he asked.

"Yes," Ellie replied. "These are the last two places I know about in the immediate region. Which means we're going to have to get a little more creative when it comes to getting supplies."

"We should all sit down and have a talk tonight

about our plans," David replied.

"Yes, we should. I can help with the plan of attack," Ellie said as she finished pulling her clothes back on.

"There's some zombies out there. I think they heard your, uh, performance."

"That wasn't a performance, that was from the heart," she replied, and pulled out her knife. "Now let's get to work."

CHAPTER THREE

The rest of the day passed with a comfortable regularity.

After getting done killing and searching the zombies that had gathered outside the cabin, he and Ellie had made it back to the campgrounds. He spent several hours helping Evelyn chop firewood and build their reserve back up.

After that, he grabbed lunch, delivered the toys to Ann, then took a shift atop the cabin nearest to the main entrance to keep an eye out. As he sat watch, he thought about what Ellie had said, thought about the people that he had agreed to watch over and care for. Maybe he hadn't fully appreciated the gravity of that situation.

Although David had done much to take more control of his own life, to become less passive and more take-charge, more active, more decisive, he had only really gotten used to making choices for himself. He had taken charge of his *own* life, and that rarely extended to more than one or two other people.

Not necessarily control, but considering how his actions might affect them. For a little while there, he'd just had to think of how his decisions would effect Evie and April. But now he had four different groups of people to look over, families, all of them with children. That was...that was a lot. And he realized that Ellie was right.

In the back of his head, he knew that he'd fight to defend them, and he had basic ideas about providing food and firewood and medicine, but he'd largely expected them to take care of themselves.

Thinking on it more, he realized that that wasn't

necessarily the wrong way to look at it, but as a community leader, he needed to have a more active role, a more direct participation in how these campgrounds were maintained and provided for. And hadn't he given himself that responsibility? Not when he and Evelyn and April had moved here, but when he had begun inviting people.

Maybe at first he was looking for, basically, roommates, but that clearly was not the case anymore. These people obviously looked to him and Evelyn and Cait for help and, to varying degrees, guidance, and protection.

The task felt daunting.

And he thought that was part of the reason it had slipped his mind. But the more he thought about it, the more powerful a motivation he felt, perhaps if only because the idea that his laziness or carelessness might result in someone getting hurt or going hungry or falling seriously ill was intolerable.

Ellie was right, he needed to be more paranoid and more desperate in his actions, but smart and controlled at the same time. Paranoia and desperation were just the fuel for the fire, the fire needed to be tended with a careful and sure hand so it didn't get out of control.

As he sat there, taking watch, he took stock of himself, and supposed that he was in a pretty decent position for this responsibility. He was young, he was fit, he had no serious injuries or ailments, either of the body or of the mind. He was a little dense sometimes, but that could be a good thing in some cases.

He had pretty good endurance, he didn't scare easy. Well, that might not be true. It was less that he didn't scare easy and more that he was finding facing bad and brutal situations, despite his terror, was easier. He didn't panic as easily, that was closer to reality. On top of that, he had a great place to live and several capable, smart, brave people to back him up and help him out. The more he thought about it, the better he felt.

Although he didn't let himself feel too good, because Ellie was also right about the world they lived in. It was brutally dangerous, and this was the most dangerous time of the year, and it was during possibly the most dangerous year the human race had ever seen. The new undead variants were brutal, efficient, and relentless.

He felt like they'd had it easy so far...for the most part. The worst they'd had to put up with at the campgrounds were some stalkers. David frowned and looked at a nearby hole in the fence surrounding the buildings. Yes, there was definitely much to do. But...David looked out over the campgrounds.

At least he was going to have a lot of help.

...

Dinner came after his watch was up. Jim had successfully bagged a deer and several rabbits, so that's what they ended up eating. Ashley's father relieved David from guard duty and he joined the others in the main office. For now, everyone tended to eat in their own places of residence.

Consequently, he sat down at a table with Evelyn, April, Cait, Ellie, and now Ashley, who had left with Ellie for another one of their 'excursions' after the two of them had returned from their own trek, and had made it back just before dinner.

As he ate dinner and talked and laughed with the others, David felt a pressure growing slowly inside of him, because he planned on having the serious discussion as soon as they were done. Partly he was a little anxious, because he wasn't sure how it was going to go.

April and Cait seemed happy to abdicate responsibility, so did Ellie, and really just do what was asked of them by David and Evelyn, and Evie herself seemed pretty amenable to the suggestions he'd made so far. But he hadn't really tried to necessarily directly step up and take charge of anything, and that's pretty much what he would be doing here.

But also he felt excited, because he largely felt (and hoped) that it would go smoothly, they would agree with him, and they could start really getting shit done.

Getting shit done felt fucking great.

"All right, David," Evelyn said after they had eaten and the conversation they'd been having had naturally fallen off for a few moments, "you've had that look on your face ever since you came back with Ellie. You want to say something. What's up?"

He chuckled nervously. "You've gotten good at reading me."

"You're easy to read," Ellie murmured.

"Yeah," Cait said.

"Definitely," Ashley agreed.

"Thanks," he replied. "Okay, anyway, serious discussion time. Ellie made a few good points, the primary one being: we aren't serious enough about running this place."

"Yeah," Evelyn murmured.

"What do you mean?" April asked.

"Yeah, fuck you Ellie, I do a lot," Cait said and stuck her tongue out at Ellie, who flipped her off.

"Eat me," she said.

"You first," Cait replied.

"Focus," David said. "I want to start involving everyone more. We need to do a lot more to build up our stores of food, clean water, and firewood, and medicine and ammo. Pretty much whatever we can get our hands on. We need to stockpile stuff, have weeks of supplies on hand in case the worst happens."

"Like what?" April murmured.

He shrugged. "I have no idea. No one could have predicted that the virus would jump to inhumans and make the world roughly fifty times more dangerous. River View's burning came out of nowhere. But basically, the more prepared we are in general, the more ready we'll be to face a crisis when it shows up on our doorstep.

"So, Evelyn, you're good at organization. Will you be willing to draw up a schedule for everyone, work with people, figure out what they think is a reasonable amount of time to offer to work and also what they're good at, what they feel comfortable doing? And drawing up a more solid guard schedule?"

"I can definitely do this. I'd love to," she replied.

"Excellent. I think we also need to start hunting more. We should go in pairs at minimum. But...before we can get serious about long-term changes and improvements to this place, we need to address the real problem. The thieves. The assholes who've been harassing everyone in the region. They need to be put down. Does anyone disagree?"

"Fuck no," Ellie muttered.

"They need to die," Cait said flatly.

"Yep," Ashley agreed.

"Agreed," Evelyn said.

He looked at April. "I mean, as much as I'm against killing people...yeah. They burned down an entire village. They gotta go. I just...I'm not sure how much I can do..."

"Don't worry, April, you won't be going along when we attack," David said.

"So you *are* attacking?" Evelyn asked.

"Some of us are, yes," he replied.

"There's not nearly enough of us," Evelyn protested.

"I know. We need help. This is a problem that's fucking with the whole region, and more than us live here. So we should ask for help," he replied, and looked at Ellie and Cait.

"We should definitely ask the farmers," Ellie said. "They've got muscle to spare, or they should. Although they might be reluctant. They're pretty insular."

"I can go to the doctors and ask them. Katya and Vanessa will want in on this, and I'm sure they'll be willing to spare at least one of them," Cait said.

"What about Jennifer?" David asked.

"Maybe. She's not as much of a fighter, but she is a wraith, so she's pretty tough..." Cait murmured.

"We should also go down to the fishing village," Ellie said.

"Where's that?" Evelyn asked.

"West of here, by the lake. It's a group of several dozen that lives among some old dockyards and fishing cabins. I'm almost sure they'll commit to our cause," Ellie explained.

"Okay. Well, that's a few different people, potentially..." Evelyn murmured.

"I want to ask those soldiers," David said.

"No," Ellie replied immediately. "We don't want,

nor need, their help."

"We could use their help," Cait said quietly.

"No! I'm not fucking going to that fucking asshole!" Ellie snapped.

"Ellie..." David said. She turned to look at him, her anger obvious, but he held her gaze, staring back at her. Finally, she let out a disgusted noise and looked away.

"Hale might help," Cait said.

"Who's Hale?" he asked.

"Lima Company's second in command. That's what they call themselves. Stern's in charge, but his second in command is a Lieutenant named Lara Hale. She's...far more diplomatic. We can probably reason with her."

"All right then. Anyone else?" he asked.

"No one I can think of," Ellie murmured after a moment. David glanced at Cait, but she shook her head.

"Okay then. So we go around, ask for help. But we definitely are missing a huge piece of the puzzle: where are these assholes hiding?" David asked.

"I've been thinking about that," Ellie replied. "I can think of three likely places. They seem to be coming from across the river, and they can't be all that far away. I've been over there, all over that place, and I'd bet that they're either in the hunting grounds, down in a valley, or in a quarry. They're all pretty decent locations to hide out. Though if I were gonna bet on it, I'd say the hunting grounds. There's a lodge and several cabins all in one area there."

"So we'll scout the locations and see what we can see," David said.

"*I'll* scout them. I'm the best scout out of all of us," Ellie said.

"I'm not letting you go alone, Ellie. And don't fucking sneak off, you agreed to help. You agreed to be a *part* of this," he replied, surprising himself as he stared across the table at her. He didn't think he'd ever taken such a firm tone with her.

She stared back at him, looking a little surprised herself.

"Fine," she said after a few seconds.

"Thank you," he replied. "Okay, we've got all the pieces figured out, how are we actually going to *do* this? I think we should ask for help first. We could hit everyone up tomorrow."

"I can go see the doctors and ask for their help, and track down Jennifer, as well. I need to go see them anyway," Cait said.

"What for?" Evelyn asked.

"Oh, um...you know...time for a checkup," she replied.

David glanced at her. That sounded like an evasion if he'd ever heard one. He considered pursuing it, but decided to let it drop. If it was important, and relevant to him, he trusted her to tell him. If not, then it wasn't exactly his business. Just because they were dating didn't mean they couldn't keep some things their own business.

"Okay," he said, "sounds good. Ellie and I will go talk to the farmers. It's about time I go visit them anyway, get some more food. Ashley, we're going to need your help. You're probably the best shot and most capable fighter out of everyone else who lives here. I want you to have a more active role in protecting this place."

She frowned. "You want me to just hang around here, playing guard?"

"Not *all* the time, but coordinate with Evelyn, set

up watches, find our weak points, figure out plans of action for emergency situations when we get attacked. I can help you with it after we get this business with the thieves settled. I know it's not exactly what you had in mind and it's not permanent, but...I'm asking you to do it. We're all going to need to pitch in," he replied.

She sighed. "Okay, fine. Yeah, I'll do it." She leaned forward. "You have to fuck me tonight, though." She looked at Evelyn. "*Both* of you."

"Deal," Evelyn replied.

"Obviously I'll do you," David said. Then he looked around the table again. "So that's it then? Cait goes for the doctors and Jennifer, then comes back here, Ellie and I go for the farmers and then come back here, then all three of us will go and ask the fishers for help, and then the military assholes. Evelyn, April, and Ashley will stay here and begin organizing a schedule and beefing up security. That sounds like a plan?"

They all agreed that it did, and he felt relief sweep over him. Well, that had gone better than he'd thought it would. Now it all had to actually *work*. Planning was easy, acting was where it got risky. But he'd have to see how it actually played out. Now that they'd gotten that out of the way, they all got up and began cleaning up the remains of their dinner.

They gathered up the bits of leftovers that remained uneaten and placed it all in a small bowl. David placed the bowl on the floor, near a little hole in the baseboard of the kitchen, and sure enough, a few moments later, a little pink nose emerged, twitched a few times, and out came Frostbite.

"He is so fucking adorable," Cait said when she saw him.

Their mouse scampered over to the bowl and began eating out of it.

"Definitely," David agreed. "I kinda wish we had a cat, but then that might cause problems. Plus...would that be weird? Would it make you feel weird?" he asked, looking at Ellie.

She shrugged. "Monkeys were a thing, although they didn't really keep them as pets, from what I hear. I don't think so. I just look like a cat, it's not like I identify with them or anything. I mean, I'm very against, you know, hurting them, but I don't see anything wrong with keeping them as pets. They seem to enjoy it, from what I've seen."

"Good to know," David replied.

They finished cleaning up and then split up, as they had a few hours left before they went to sleep. Evelyn and Ashley sat down and began some preliminary work on setting up a schedule, and April headed up to her room, as did Ellie, to her and Cait's shared bedroom.

Cait, however, tracked him down as he was on his way to give April her books. He was on his way up to the third floor when he heard her whisper his name from the base of the stairs.

"Yeah?" he asked, turning around.

"Get your ass down here," she snapped softly.

She looked...excited. He could see down her shirt from this angle. "Okay."

He walked back down and as soon as he was close enough, she took his hand and quickly guided him off to the room next to the kitchen that they had yet to make real use of. He had an idea to turn it into an armory, but for now it was packed full of tables and chairs. They'd done a bit to organize it, making sure nothing was hiding among the stored furniture, but not much.

"Yes?" he asked as she pushed the door most of the way closed.

The only light now came in the form of moonlight spilling in through the window. She looked eerily beautiful as she stared at him. Cait answered by pressing her lips to his and that pulse of hungry desire was right there, and he didn't just want her, he fucking *needed her.*

He grabbed her and hugged her tightly to him, kissing her back firmly, and she moaned in response. He kissed harder and pushed her back up against the nearest wall, knocking over one of the chairs in the process.

"Oh!" she said, startled, then laughed, then resumed kissing him.

He got his hand up under the t-shirt she was wearing. She wasn't wearing anything beneath it. He groaned as he took one of her big, firm breasts in his grasp and began groping it. It only intensified his hungry need for her.

Behind them, in the middle of the room, was a pretty sturdy desk. He turned around, grabbing her and bringing her around, and she let out a little squeal of delight as he did so.

"Get your fucking pants off," he growled, undoing the button on her cargo pants as he walked her back towards the desk.

"Yes, *sir,*" she murmured, kissed him once more, then quickly pulled her pants down.

She'd also opted out of panties, as she often seemed to. She barely managed to fold up her pants and set them down where her ass would go, given the desk would be cold, before he picked her up and sat her down on it.

"Get your fucking legs open," he said as he undid his zipper and quickly began getting his cock out, just like he'd done with Ellie.

"Yes, sir," she panted, and leaned back, putting her hands behind her to support her. She raised her legs and spread them out, and in the moonlight he could just make out her glistening, slick pussy, ready to get fucked. As soon as he was out, David stepped back up to her and slipped his rigid dick inside of her.

She let out a long, loud moan as she took it into herself. He grabbed her and kissed her hard as he started fucking her, sliding his cock smoothly in and out of her, groaning at the immediately intense wave of pure bliss that was her vagina.

"*Yesssss, David...*" she moaned loudly between kisses. "I fucking...oh God...I fucking *missed you today...*" she groaned and wrapped her legs around him.

He held her tightly to him and started going harder and faster. "I missed you too, Cait. Oh my fucking God, I missed you so much."

"Come on, give it to me, honey. Give me that fat cock," she moaned.

He reached down and yanked her shirt up and she leaned back a little, letting him get it up over her big tits. They looked beyond amazing, firm and pale, bouncing wonderfully as they fucked. He looked down between them, staring at her amazing body, looking past her tits, down to her thick, pale thighs and his cock, disappearing into her sweet, pink pussy again and again. He was going to blow the biggest fucking load inside of her.

"I can't fuck for long," she panted, and he looked back up at her achingly beautiful face. "Gotta pull guard duty. That's why I-*ah!*-why I did this."

"You're gonna be up all night *and* go to the doctors?" he asked, then groaned as she squeezed him with her legs, pushing him all the way inside of her.

"No babe, Jim's gonna take over for me at two in the morning, then I'll get some sleep, then I'll get up and go. I'll be fine, don't you worry about me. I can take care of myself," she said, grinning, her eyes wide and full of lust. "Now fucking come in me. I want to feel you fucking orgasming inside me. I want all of it in me."

"Oh fucking...oh Cait..." he moaned, hammering away at her pussy.

There were no more words for the rest of the short session, just grunting and panting and moaning, and then he was coming, and she let out a cry of her own as she began to orgasm shortly after he triggered.

He pumped her sweet human pussy full of his seed, emptying his nuts into her one, hard contraction at a time, shooting his load into her in thick spurts. He filled her up, just like she'd demanded, and felt her coming all over the front of his pants and his dick.

He listened to her inarticulate moans and grunts of pleasure, stared into her beautiful blue eyes, bare inches from his as she stared back, both of them locked in the unified bliss of mutual orgasm. They both held each other tightly until they had finished coming.

"Oh wow...fuck..." David whispered as he leaned against her, and she against him, both of them getting their breaths back.

"God*damn* do I love your cock," she groaned as he pulled out of her. She put a hand over herself, then sighed. "This is the problem with you busting your fucking nut in me."

She got up and turned around, then began sorting

through her pockets with her other hand. He looked down at her ass as he began to button himself back up, but then gave up, because he was going to have to change his pants and boxers anyway.

Fuck, she had a fat ass.

She found her rag and began cleaning herself up. While she did that, he just took his pants and his boxers off, since her sex juices were already getting cold. "I gotta go change, babe."

"Okay," she said, finishing up. She tugged her shirt back down into place, then started getting her pants on. "Give me a kiss, I've gotta go get ready for guard duty."

He kissed her, then left her to it, heading back out into the hallway. He looked around, wondering if anyone had come to listen. Probably someone had, and had snuck off in the interval of time between now and when the sex had actually finished. Probably Ellie. Usually, whenever sex was happening, someone came to watch or listen.

Or jump in.

He headed upstairs, holding his clothes, and got back into his and Evie's bedroom. He took the stuff he carried around in his pockets and on his belt out and set it on his dresser, then tossed the dirty clothes into a pile that he needed to wash very soon.

He went over to the washbasin and quickly washed himself off, then pulled on a fresh set of undershorts and cargo pants. After replacing his gear, he moved over to his backpack and dug out the three books he'd managed to find. With these in hand, he stepped back out into the hallway and moved over to April's door, which was open a crack. He knocked on it.

"Come in," she said.

He pushed it open and found her laying in bed, reading by candlelight. "Hello, beautiful," he said, stepping in and pushing the door mostly shut behind him.

"Hi," she replied, smiling and setting her book aside. "What's up?"

"I brought you some presents," he replied, crossing the room to stand beside the bed. He pulled the three books out from behind his back and handed them to her.

"Holy shit, thank you!"

She took them from him and looked over them, a true and honest happiness lighting up her face. He never saw her as happy as when she was looking over a brand new book, and that alone was worth hunting for them. Though before long, he saw her smile falter, and she looked up at him, a little nervous.

"Everything okay?" he asked.

"Yeah. Yes. I just...normally I know we have sex when you bring me these and I'm kinda...I'm not feeling it right now..." she murmured.

"April," he said, and crouched down beside the bed, then took one of her hands. "You don't *have* to do anything sexual with me. I don't want you to *ever* feel like you *must* do that. You should only have sex or give oral or whatever when you want to..." he hesitated. "You haven't been having sex with me when you don't want to, have you?" he asked, suddenly worried. He didn't think so, he thought he would've been able to pick up on that...

"No, no, David," she replied, setting the books aside and gently squeezing his hand. "No, so far, all the times we've fucked, it's because I wanted to."

He studied her for a moment, then nodded, feeling relieved. He believed her. "I don't want you to ever feel pressured."

"I don't. You've been really good to me. I mean really, I just feel bad. I know how much you love sex, and I want to make you feel good, you know...reward you, for all the nice things you do," she explained.

"Sex is always appreciated, but I don't want you feeling like you owe me. I do nice things for you because I want to. I want to make you happy. This relationship is going fine, April, just the way it is now."

"Okay...I *would* like it if you laid with me for a little while," she said.

"I'd like that too," he replied, and she shifted aside and raised the blankets for him. He took off his boots and got in next to her, then wrapped his arms around her and hugged her to him. She hugged him back, burying her face in his chest.

"I want you to know," she said, her voice a little muffled, "that you're the best boyfriend I've ever had. Honestly, you're the nicest man who has ever been in my life. And Evie and Cait are the nicest women. You three have changed my life."

"I'm sorry that it was miserable before, but I'm glad we could help you so much," he replied, hugging her a little more tightly.

She felt good to hold, felt good and comfortable in his arms, pressing herself against him. A few of the nights he'd come in here and slept with her all night, holding her like this, or pressing up against her back, and she always seemed to respond so well to it, like it was the thing she wanted most in the world.

"It sucked before, but before is over, and nothing can change before. Right now is what matters. At least that's what Cait tells me. She's right, but it's hard to really, you know, believe it. I mean like fully.

The shit from before...it left scars. But Cait's helping a lot."

"You two seem to be getting along really well," David replied.

"We are." She paused, then pulled her head back slightly and looked up at him. "You aren't jealous...are you?"

"No, not at all," he replied, and he kissed her forehead. "I'm happy. I'm thrilled. I want the two of you to get along. I want us all to get along. I love where this is going, and how well we get along with each other."

"That's good. I'm sorry to keep asking, keep checking on stuff like that, I just...get nervous. Because it's like my brain keeps telling me, every day, over and over, that you're all lying, and you really hate me, or you're just putting up with me, or maybe it's good now, but it's going to get fucked up. I'm just so fucking insecure. I'm sorry."

"It's okay, I know how you feel," he said. "I've definitely got insecurities of my own. Evie does. Even Cait and Ellie do. They're just...better at hiding it." He sighed softly. "I don't really know what advice to give you."

"Cait told me...just don't feed it. That's what she said. She said, when that voice speaks up, and tells you what a failure you are, ignore it. Don't feed it. I told her sometimes it's impossible to ignore, and even when it's not it's *so* hard. She said it gets easier over time. I just have to keep doing it. Keep practicing, like any other skill."

"That makes sense," he murmured. She put her head back down against his chest and he rubbed the back of her neck, feeling her dry, scaly skin against his own. "I think it might help, living among people who care about you, who like you, who help you, in a place where your skills and contributions will be valued."

"I'm really hoping that's true," she replied. "I *have* been feeling better since running into you. I guess it's kind of like I've been sick for a really long time, and I'm finally getting medicine, and it's going to take a while for it to work and for me to fully heal up. And I'll certainly have some permanent damage..."

"I hope not," he murmured. "I just want you to be happy."

She laughed and squeezed him. "You're helping a lot with that." She yawned. "Fuck, part of the reason I'm not in the mood is because I'm so *tired.*"

"I've been meaning to ask...should I be more worried about that?"

"No. Mainly it's...have I mentioned this already? I can't remember now. Reps kind of go into hibernation mode a little during the winter, because of our physiology. I get very low energy, very sleepy, and I'll stay that way for months, until spring, basically. It sucks. So don't worry, if there's something to worry about, I'll let you know."

"Okay."

"Thank you for the books, David. Really. They're...just the best."

"You're welcome, April. I'm happy they make you so happy."

He could tell from her voice that she was getting very sleepy. After a little while, she shifted back up and laid her head on the pillow, beside his. She looked at him for another minute or so with her tired eyes, and then she was out.

He laid there for a little bit longer with her, and

then carefully pulled himself up and out of her bed, kissed her gently on the forehead, then blew out her candle and quietly exited the room, closing her door almost all the way.

He knew she liked it open a crack. Fuck, at this point, they all did.

From there, he went back to his room and gathered up his and Evelyn's dirty clothes, and took them down to the basement, where they'd set up a basic clothes-washing station. It wasn't great, but it was better than just continuing to wear filthy clothes.

Especially considering some of them were practically biohazards. He spent an hour washing and wringing out their shirts and pants and underclothes, and then hung them up on the lines they'd draped from the ceiling.

Once that was done, he headed back upstairs and took a moment to check all the windows and doors. They were secure, or as secure as they were going to get, and everything seemed to be in order. Heading up to the second story, he saw that Evelyn and Ashley had since left the kitchen. They were probably waiting for him upstairs.

He saw the door to Ellie's and Cait's shared room was partially open, and there was still some light, so he walked over and knocked on it gently.

"Yeah?" Ellie asked.

"I just came to say goodnight," he replied, poking his head in. She was laying on the bed wearing nothing but panties with her hands behind her head.

She smiled at him. "I heard some of your conversation with April."

He sighed. "That was private."

"I'm sorry," she replied, and she did sound sorry.

"It's just...you were right above me, and I have great hearing, I-I didn't mean to, I just did. I just wanted to say, you're an amazingly sweet man, and I'm so glad you're with Cait."

"Really? Any specific reason?"

She sighed softly. "Cait's tough. Tougher than me, in some ways, but a lot less in others. She deserves someone like you. Someone who will respect her, and work hard for her, to make her happy. I think she wants it, maybe even needs it, more than she'll ever admit."

He crossed his arms. "You don't think the same could be said about you?"

"..maybe," she admitted reluctantly. "But this isn't about me. It's about you. And Cait. Oh, and I wanted to let you know, if you hurt her, emotionally, because she could kick your ass, I'll break you, David. Do you understand?"

"I think you've said something like that to me already, and yes, I understand."

She frowned. "I'm sorry, I just get...protective. And I've seen too many men rip hearts out. If it helps, I believe you won't ever try to hurt her."

"Yeah," he said after a moment, "that helps...goodnight, Ellie."

"Goodnight, David." She paused. "Give me a kiss?"

He crossed the room and leaned down and kissed her on the lips. She gave him a nice kiss back, then reached out, took his hand, and laid it across her bare, furry breast.

"Don't be afraid to slip into my bed in the middle of the night, yeah? I admit, I might give you a rap on the head if you startle me, but this pussy's worth it, right?"

"Yeah, it is," he admitted.

She laughed. "Knew it."

He gave her breast a gentle squeeze, then left the room and headed upstairs. He heard quiet conversation as he approached his bedroom, and as he walked in, he saw that he was right: Evelyn and Ashley were laying in his bed together, nude.

"Well, it's about time," Ashley said.

"Sorry, I had to say goodnight to people and fuck Cait and check on April," he replied as he pushed the door most of the way closed, then began to take his clothes off.

"Is she okay?" Evelyn asked.

"Yeah, she's fine. She's sleeping now. And Ellie's headed to bed, too. Cait is on guard for now. How did the planning go?" he asked.

"Great, I think," Evelyn replied.

"Yeah, tomorrow we get to go around and ask people 'what don't you suck fucking dick at doing?'" Ashley said.

"I'll be doing the talking to everyone but your family, apparently," Evelyn murmured. "God, you can be so tactless sometimes."

"Okay, I wasn't *literally* going to say that to people!" Ashley cried.

"Of course," David said as he finished stripping and moved over to the washbasin where he cleaned himself up one more time for the night, given he was going to be fucking and more than likely one of the two women would be putting his junk in their mouths.

"I think tomorrow will be a very productive day," Evelyn said. "I'll speak with everyone, get an idea of what they're good at, what they're comfortable doing, what sort of skills they're going to be willing to learn.

I'm assuming that you're going to want to continue with our idea of a twenty four hour a day guard cycle?"

"Yeah," he replied. "Definitely." He finished washing and drying, then walked over to the bed. It was enormous, about seven feet wide and nine long. They'd laid out three mattresses side-by-side, given it was the easiest way to make something with enough length to handle Evie's seven and a half foot tall body.

They made room for him as he climbed onto the bed and laid down in between them. It still felt really weird to do this, sometimes. Obviously a good weird. Weird in the sense that, before he'd met Evie and April and the other women now in his life, he had a far, far lower amount of success when it came to matters of love and sex.

And now, since he had first hooked up with Evie, he didn't think there had actually been a single day that had gone by where he hadn't had sex at least once, and often he was hooking up with more than one woman, all of whom were extremely attractive. It felt more than a little like a dream.

He looked at both of them. Evie in all her buxom, huge glory, with her huge breasts and enormous hips and thighs and her wonderful extra padding. Ashley, skinny and trim and very fit, her skin pale, and her hot tattoos.

Because she was his girlfriend, he kissed her first, putting his lips to hers and laying a hand across one of her huge breasts. There was something wonderfully erotic about groping a breast that was not just too big to fully get your hand around, but way too big.

Everything about her was huge. He'd always

fantasized about having a goliath lover in his life, but he'd also always worried that he wouldn't be able to satisfy her. He was very glad to find that the size difference didn't seem to matter.

Unless she was consistently and effectively faking, sex seemed to be a very mutually satisfying experience. He knew for sure it was for him.

She kissed him with a happy passion, running one large hand up and down his back with a slow sensuality. They were still figuring the relationship out, but certainly they were much more settled than they had been a few weeks ago.

They were getting used to each other, discovering each other, figuring out the best way to fit together. He knew that she was sensitive about her size, as she'd spent the majority of her life around people who were noticeably smaller than her, and her great size had either been a point of cruel ridicule or fear.

He was doing everything he could think of to reassure her that he was genuinely happy with her as she was. Obviously, certain things had to be taken into consideration, mainly how easy it was for her to accidentally injure him or April or Cait, or anyone else they took into their bed, but she was good about it.

Evelyn made out with him for a few moments before passing him off to Ashley, who was growing impatient at his back. She had reached around him and taken his cock into her grasp while she waited, massaging it slowly and kissing the back of his neck. He finally rolled over and kissed her, and she responded eagerly in kind, pushing her slim, fit body against his own.

He reached back and grabbed her ass, her

wonderful, firm, toned ass. Ashley laughed happily as she shoved her tongue into his mouth, and he found that he loved how fully and freely she threw herself into the sex whenever they had it, or he watched her having it with someone else.

She was a very enthusiastically erotic woman.

Ashley broke the kiss suddenly. "Lemme ride your tongue," she said in a rush.

"All right," he replied. He looked over at Evie. "Would you mind putting your mouth to work?"

"Not at all, honey," she replied.

She gave him a kiss, then began to shift. David shifted as well, getting onto his back, and Ashley quickly straddled his face. He reached up and settled his hands on her thighs, running them up and down her smooth, hot skin, feeling her firm muscles beneath.

He stuck his tongue out, getting the tip between her lips, and began to gently massage her clit with it. She let out a low moan and reached out, placing her hands against the wall. Within a few seconds, he let out his own groan as Evie got to work and took his whole cock into her mouth slowly between her lips.

That was something else really great about dating a goliath: she had a pretty big mouth. She was excellent at giving really good head.

He worked Ashley's clit with his tongue with small, firm strokes, caressing it slowly, knowing how much she liked that. He liked how much he had gotten to know these women sexually as well as emotionally.

He was slowly figuring out the right ways in which to pleasure the women in his life, the nuances, subtle variations, and specifics that worked best with each of them. And they seemed to like to learn him as well. Especially Evie. She was doing such a wonderful job, filling him with such intense pleasure as she slowly sucked his cock, putting her lips to such pleasurable use. He felt positively alight with sexual energy.

Especially when, after several more minutes of oral pleasure, Evelyn straightened up and said, "Okay, let's switch. I'll take over oral duty and you can ride *my* tongue while David fucks me."

"Oh hell yes," Ashley replied, getting off of him. "Your tongue is the best tongue." She glanced down at him. "No offense."

"None taken, her mouth is fantastic," he replied as he got up.

Evelyn just smiled as she laid down on her back and opened her legs for him. As he settled in between her tremendous thighs, Ashley swung her own legs back over Evelyn's face, straddling her now, and she let out a loud moan of pleasure as she began to put her tongue to good use.

He slipped his cock into Evelyn's pussy and groaned loudly. She was always so fucking wet inside. He grabbed her huge hips as he began sliding in and out of her, the pleasure burning into him with an immediate intensity.

He listened to her muffled moans of sexual gratification as he stared as Ashley's fit, pale ass. He loved the way she slowly moved her hips, the movements careful and deliberate, a gradual grind back and forth as she worked with Evelyn.

His eyes drifted lower, to Evie's huge tits, which were gently swaying in sync with his thrusting. David started to go harder, wanting to see them move more, and soon they were bouncing as Evelyn let out louder groans and grunts of pleasure. All three of them moaned in mutual satisfaction.

Before long, he laid his thumb against Evie's clit and began to stimulate it, rubbing it firmly, and she let out a cry of pleasure.

"Damn, what are you doing back-ah!-back there?" Ashley asked.

"What I always do," he replied and went harder and faster, both with his thumb and his cock.

Evelyn let out a loud, muffled cry and he wondered if it would wake April up. He hoped not. Maybe it would just give her sexy dreams. Within another ten seconds he had his goliath girlfriend orgasming, and how fucking wonderful that felt.

Somehow, he managed to hold onto his own orgasm as he felt her vaginal muscles clenching and fluttering wildly around his cock and her release of hot sex juices. He fucked her throughout the whole thing, making her cry out intensely. They kept going until she had finished.

"Can we fuck now?" Ashley asked. "I can return the oral favor," she added, looking down at Evelyn.

"I'm okay with that," David replied.

"Mmm-hmm," Evelyn agreed.

He pulled out of her and shifted back. Evelyn remained where she was, her eyes closed, looking very pleased and satisfied from her orgasm. Ashley got onto her hands and knees between Evelyn's huge thighs and put her face down into her crotch. David got up against her firm, fit backside, running his hands slowly over her tight ass, and settled them on her hips.

"Don't hold back," Ashley said, and then began to eat Evelyn out.

He didn't hold back.

David slipped inside of her wonderfully tight

pussy, which was incredibly wet now from all the oral she'd been getting, tightened his grip on her hips, and started hammering away at that sweet, sweet pussy of hers.

"Oh, *fuck,* Ash," he groaned as he pounded her.

She moaned in response and pushed against him. He gripped her hips more tightly, digging in his fingertips, and fucked the hell out of her. And he found out that she was primed to pop from all the foreplay. Hardly a minute went by before she began to come all over his dick, and he groaned, leaning forward, hunched over her as the pleasure slammed into him.

He began to come inside of her, and found himself thinking of the unbelievable position he found himself in: this was the *fourth* woman he had orgasmed inside of today. And without protection. He was finding that to be a clear distinction. Not that he would have complained if any of them had insisted on using protection.

But oh good fucking lord the pleasure of coming into bare pussy.

David was once again awash in the sea of mindless, orgasmic bliss as he drained his cock into Ashley's pussy, feeling her climax along with him, listening to her moans of ecstasy and rapture. He came what he had left inside of him and then he was finished, left sweaty and panting and exhausted, and he pulled out of her and laid down beside Evelyn.

She giggled. "Are you okay, dear?"

"Just perfect," David groaned in reply. He knew he should probably wash himself off, but he was fast fading into sleep now.

He got beneath the blankets.

"What about you? Are you okay, pretty girl?"

Evelyn asked.

"Very much okay," Ashley murmured. She was laying on Evelyn now, who was gently running her hand up and down Ashley's smooth, pale back. "Can I sleep here? My parents will probably bitch at me tomorrow morning but I think they'd bitch at me a whole lot more if I came home smelling like dick and sex."

Evelyn giggled again. "Yes, Ashley. You can sleep here with us."

She yawned. "Thank you. I'll take that sleep right about now."

She rolled off of Evelyn and the two women joined David beneath the blankets.

And then he crashed headlong and happily into sleep.

CHAPTER FOUR

Despite everything, despite the fact that he was walking through a frozen forest infested with the undead and he had possibly the most enormous task of his life looming before him, David felt good.

Freshly fucked, freshly cleaned, with a meal in his stomach and his favorite clothes on, he walked across the recently fallen snow with Ellie at his side. It was morning, the sun up for only maybe two hours, and they were off to see the farmers.

Cait was still sleeping when they left, but Evelyn promised to get her up within the next half hour, and he trusted her. He trusted both of them. They were both competent professionals when they wanted to be, and knew to treat this situation and the tasks before them with proper seriousness.

David studied the landscape around him as they struck out eastbound. He saw snow, patches of dirt, dead trees and skeletal bushes dotting the area. The sun beamed down on it all from a cloudless blue sky. His gaze settled on Ellie, who wore a simple t-shirt and dark cargo pants. Her fur must keep her so warm.

He decided to ask her something that had been bugging him all morning now.

"Ellie?"

"Yes?"

"I was curious...both you and Cait have brought it up now, and so I wanted to ask: who else is part of this mysterious 'group' of yours?"

She hesitated. "Our group?"

"Yeah. Whenever you or Cait showed me one of your hideouts, you explained that you shared it with a small group of people similar to yourselves. So far,

I've only met, or even heard of, you and Cait. And I thought, more people like the two of you would be very useful right about now," he explained to her.

"Oh. Yes. That." She hesitated further. "Don't tell anyone, but it's just us now."

"What? What happened?"

She sighed. "Life happened. In the way that it does nowadays. One of them was a man, another jag, and he was killed by a pack of stalkers a while ago. Another was a female human, and she ended up picking up and leaving. One of them was the goliath that I mentioned works with the doctors, Vanessa. I mean, she's still *around,* just that she basically settled down. She'll be helping, I hope.

"Another one, a guy, a rep, he flaked on us, disappeared. Don't really know what happened to him, but he was always kind of skittish. I think he'd just had enough. Or, fuck, maybe we'll find his body out there. Cait and I certainly looked, but his stuff was gone and there wasn't any evidence anywhere of foul play...but this *is* a big region." She sighed again, more sadly. "But yeah, it's really just the two of us." She paused. "Fuck, I guess it's just me, now that Cait's settling down."

"I doubt Cait's settling down," David replied. "Just because she's dating me–"

"No...it's not just that. Something's different about her. I'm not sure what, but the fact that she's been hanging around the campgrounds so much is indicative of that."

"It seems like you're training Ashley to be like you," he said after a moment, realizing that she might actually have a point.

"Ashley said that was your idea."

"Yeah, I suggested it to her. She wanted to leave,

but was desperate to help her family. I thought it was a fair compromise, living across the land, being able to drop in almost every day, spend the night every now and then."

"Wish you would've mentioned it to me before dumping her in my lap," Ellie groused.

David rolled his eyes. "Give me a break, you and Cait fucking love her."

"Yeah, okay, fair point. She's great. She reminds me a lot of me, just...without the damage. Or, really, without as much. Everyone has damage now. I find the idea of teaching her, showing her the land, training her in new combat techniques and lifestyle changes, very appealing. And she's so willing, happy even, to listen."

"You're welcome," David said.

She sighed heavily. "Whatever." They walked for a bit longer. "So...April was certainly, uh, enthusiastic this morning."

He chuckled and felt heat rushing up his neck to his cheeks. "You heard that, huh?"

"I think everyone heard that."

"Yeah, she was more, uh, horny than usual. I guess she got a good, long sleep. I came in to check on her and she was awake and she made me get in bed with her and she fucking rode me."

"I bet she's really tight. She's so skinny. Even skinner than Ashley is," Ellie murmured.

"Oh my God, *yes*. She is *so* fucking tight," David replied.

"All right, all right, shut it. We're almost there, got to be professional," Ellie said.

He realized he could see the top of the tallest building, a silo, through the trees now, and within a few moments, they were coming out of the woods, approaching the front gate. Two guards sat there around a fire in a metal barrel.

"Ellie. David," one of them, a man David had gotten to know over the past few weeks named Oliver, said.

"Oliver," Ellie replied with a short nod. "Need to talk to the boss."

"What about?" he asked, sitting up a little straighter.

"Something big. I'd rather keep it between him and us for now," she replied.

Oliver looked at them closely, then glanced at the other guard, then finally got to his feet. "All right, I'll go get him."

He got up and began heading back to the main farmhouse. David looked out over the fields on the farmland, dead and dry and covered in snow. Farther back, he could see three rectangular buildings of glass that he'd come to realize were hydroponic gardens. He had to get one of those for himself. The ability to grow their own vegetables would be fantastic.

A few minutes went by in the cold and finally Oliver reemerged, trailed by the man in charge, William Thatch. He looked tired, then again, it seemed like he always looked tired.

He stopped about halfway down the path between the front gate and then motioned for the two of them to join him.

"Let them in!" Oliver called as he started walking back.

They passed the gate guard and made their way down the pathway, passing Oliver as he made his way back to his post, where he stood and waited, watching them closely. They met William in the middle.

"Good to see you Ellie, David. Now, what's so

important that it demands my personal attention?" he asked, sounding amicable enough, but David thought he could detect an undercurrent of something else. Anxiety? Frustration? Distraction, at least.

"We're going after the assholes who burned down River View and have been harassing the region for the past month. We'd like help," David replied simply.

William looked first surprised, and then reluctant, and then a little guilty, and even before he opened his mouth to respond, David knew that he was going to say no.

"As much as you and I are in agreement about your intended goal, I'm afraid I'm not currently in a position to offer any kind of assistance," he admitted.

"Not even one man and one gun?" Ellie asked.

"I'm afraid not."

"Is something wrong? We might be able to help," David asked.

He pursed his lips. "I've said all I'm willing to say," he replied firmly, which made David think that they did indeed have something else going on, but he supposed he understood. It was an issue of trust. If he admitted vulnerability, it could be taken advantage of. Probably he didn't think that David or Ellie would use the information against him, probably, but they might let it slip. That was the problem with knowledge: once you passed it on, you had no control over its spread. And people, in general, were bad at keeping secrets.

"I *am* sorry," he said after a moment of silence passed, and sighed out a cloud of breath in the cold air. "I genuinely do wish I could help. I want them gone as much as you do. And..." Now he looked reluctant. "I could use a favor."

"You're turning us down *and* you want a favor?" Ellie asked.

"Ellie," David said, and she sighed and crossed her arms, but held her peace. "What is it, Mister Thatch?"

"One of our own has gone missing. He's young, hardheaded, gone off half-cocked on some stupid run into the wilderness. God knows why. I spoke to his older brother and got a likely location where he might have run off to. Would you be so good as to bring him back? I'll give you double what we normally pay out."

"When did he leave?"

"A few hours ago, just after sunrise," William replied.

David sighed, considering it. Did they have time? He supposed it didn't matter. They needed the food. "We'll do it. Where is he?"

"To the east, at an abandoned farm maybe two miles beyond the abandoned train station."

"I know where that is," Ellie said. "We'll find him, one way or another, and get him back here promptly."

"I do thank you for this. It is genuinely appreciated. Oh, and, his name is Tyler."

"I'm glad we could help. We'll be back soon."

"Good luck."

They began walking away, back towards the exit.

. . .

"You're changing, you know that?" Ellie asked.

They'd hardly said anything as they had walked east, eventually passing the abandoned train station where he and Cait had fought off a pack of rippers in the darkness. He still had fucking nightmares about that, sometimes.

"What do you mean?" he replied, glancing back briefly at the train station as it disappeared behind another treeline.

"That was pretty smooth. Pretty diplomatic. You know it's smarter to keep good relations with them, even at an inconvenience."

"We need the food," David replied.

"We do. You could have said 'thanks but no thanks, we've got better things to do'. But you didn't. I would've, because I was pissed."

"You get too pissed, Ellie," he murmured.

"I know. That's another thing. You actually stood up to me last night about scouting. You genuinely caught me off guard with that. It was impressive."

"Well...I need your help. I *want* your help. And, you know, I want to help you, too. I want to be there when you do stuff like that."

"Don't make the mistake of thinking that I need you, David," Ellie replied, a little harshly, he thought.

"I didn't say that," he murmured. She didn't say anything, and after a few moments of feeling a familiar frustration beginning to well up within him, he stopped suddenly. She stopped as well after a few steps, and reluctantly looked back at him. "What's your problem?" he asked finally, staring into her yellow cat eyes. "What's your deal, Ellie? Do you like me or not? Do you trust me or not? Do you want to be around me or not?"

These were questions he'd wanted to ask her, point blank, almost since they'd had their first real interaction. He hadn't, because they were too direct and probably rude, and also because he was waiting for them to go away.

Only they hadn't, because shit like this kept happening.

"I...do like you, David. I mean, I thought that was obvious. We've had sex more than once now and–"

He cut her off. "And what does that mean? I know you can sleep with people you don't *like,* Ellie."

"I trust you!" she snapped. "I've shared things with you that I haven't shared with anyone outside of Cait and Jennifer, okay? I like you, I trust you, I want to be around you."

"Then why is it like pulling teeth to get you to say that? Why does it seem like you have to punctuate every fifth sentence with something meant to forcibly remind me of the distance between us? I swear we can't go a day of interaction without you tossing a bucket of ice water over a conversation," he asked.

She sighed and looked down for a moment. "It isn't *you,* David."

"So you do this with Cait? With Jennifer?" he asked.

She looked up again, like she was going to jump to her defense, then hesitated. "It's not...the same. With them," she murmured.

"So it *is* different? I'm right, then, yes? I mean, if I'm doing something to piss you off, then tell me to my face. You obviously don't have a problem with shit like that."

"You're being surprisingly mean, David," she said, and *that* was like a bucket of ice water across him. She sounded and looked shockingly vulnerable, and he felt a surge of guilt.

He sighed softly and pinched the bridge of his nose, massaging it for a moment. "I'm sorry, Ellie...I'm sorry," he murmured.

"No, you're right. I just...wasn't ready for this. You're right and you've got a right to be frustrated, I suppose. I...don't really want to get into it. Suffice to say, I like you, and that scares me," she replied.

"*Why?*" he asked, exasperated.

"I...don't want to talk about it," she replied, looking guilty now.

He stared at her for a moment, and his frustration quickly began to melt away. Now he just felt bad. "Okay," he said, "that's...fair. That's your right. I'm...fuck, I'm sorry I brought this up at all. Let's just go."

"David," she said, and crossed the distance between them, and put her hands on his shoulders. "I'm not...attacking you. I'm not punishing you. This isn't a *you* thing, per se. It's about you, but honestly, it's more about *me* and *my* problems. And I...need time, to think about if I even want to get into...the whole thing."

"All right, I get that," David replied. "I'm sorry I got upset. And it's fine, if you don't want to tell me, it's really fine, I won't be angry. I just...wanted things to be...nicer, between us."

"They are," she murmured, and she hugged him. "But I hear you. I will...*try*."

"I appreciate that," he replied, hugging her back. After a few seconds, he sighed. "We really should be hurrying."

"Yes, we should," she agreed.

They disengaged and began hurrying off through the woods.

"So what is this place?" he asked after a few moments.

"Like William said, an abandoned farm. There's a farmhouse, a barn, a silo, but that collapsed, and some sheds and fields. I found it a few months back when I was scouting out here. Tried to search it but I was run off."

"By what?"

"Rippers."

David didn't say anything, just felt his stomach go cold as he flashed back to running into that pack of fucking monsters in the train station. Cait had saved his ass. It had been worth it, they'd found a good cache of supplies there, including the submachine gun that he now had with him, slung over his neck. He'd ended up taking it today, though he wasn't entirely sure why. Just a feeling. Apparently his feeling was correct.

The pair of them kept walking until finally they broke through another treeline and came out into a large, snowy clearing where this abandoned farm sat. It looked a lot like the one they'd just come from, only derelict and dead.

Although, David saw as he studied the area, not too dead. There were footprints in the snow, leading towards the main house. They were steady prints, in a roughly straight line, with boots. Almost certainly not an undead, zombie or any of the newer types. *Someone* was here, at least. Ellie began making her way forward after a bit.

"Come on," she murmured. "Be careful."

"Yep," David replied softly, gripping his SMG and double-checking that the safety was off. They made their way along the center of the snowy field. He spied the broken remains of the silo off to the right, fallen in on itself in a heap of broken rubble. Surrounding them was a wooden fence that looked in surprisingly good condition. It all did, actually, for being abandoned.

"How long has this place been empty?" he asked quietly, scanning back and forth for any signs of life.

"Not very long," Ellie replied. "I don't know for sure, but from the way people talked about it, maybe a year or two. Not sure what happened to force whoever lived here out."

David began to say something, but then they heard a shout and several gunshots coming from the farmhouse. In one of the second story windows, he saw that telltale flashing of muzzle flare. Ellie took off. "That's our cue!"

He followed after her, adrenaline flooding his body. *Please don't let it be rippers...* he thought miserably. He hated fighting them so much. He thought he saw dark movement somewhere to the right of the house, near the back, but then they were too close to the house and it was out of sight. It had happened so fast he couldn't be sure if it was a shadow or not. Well, he'd find out one way or another.

David followed Ellie as she came up onto the front porch. The front door was cracked open, and apparently she thought there was no need for subtlety, because she kicked it open and aimed her pistol into the room beyond.

Overhead, more shouting and gunfire.

"Clear!" Ellie called, and rushed in.

They moved through a living room full of dusty furniture and into a hallway. Something growled off to their left, and he knew in that instant that yes, they were indeed facing rippers.

"Fuck!" he snapped as he saw two of them scrambling in through a smashed-open back door, right into the hallway.

He also just caught sight of one scrambling up

some stairs right next to them.

"Go! Go! I got this!" he yelled as he leveled the SMG at the two coming in.

Ellie didn't wait, rushing up the stairs and opening fire.

David focused on the two monstrous things coming at him, aiming for them. He had to kill them damned quick. The sleek, dark creatures, reps turned into undead, given razor-sharp talons and nasty teeth, advanced on him with shrieking hisses. He unloaded on them, hosing them down with the submachine gun.

The first spray of gunfire was the most concentrated, and it caught the closest creature in the chest, neck, and face, splattering the hallway with dark blood and shreds of flesh. The second one ducked and began sprinting for him, and he saw it preparing to leap as he readjusted aim and squeezed the trigger again.

The volley of red hot lead hit it just in time, splitting its skull and spraying its brains across the walls. It dropped just a few feet from his feet. David let out a sharp breath, preparing to hurry up after Ellie, when another shadow fell across the ground outside the back door. A second later, another ripper came screaming in after him.

He fired off the rest of his bullets, depleting the magazine, and cut it down, ending it with two well-placed rounds in whatever it had left for brains. He hastily reloaded, hands shaking slightly, waiting for the next thing to happen.

Nothing did. He heard another shout and a gunshot from overhead, then silence. He cursed, glancing down at his SMG. He only had the one reload. Letting it hang, he pulled out his pistol and jogged up the stairs.

"Ellie!?" he called.

A pause, then, "Here, David! I'm okay, so is the survivor. Help me secure the area!"

"On it! Coming up!"

He hurried up the stairs and poked his head into the first room he saw. This was where Ellie and the survivor, a wide-eyed man with trembling hands and a shaved head, stood. The man was panting. David locked eyes with him. "You're Tyler?"

The man stared back, getting his breath back, shaking badly. "Y-yeah," he managed after a few seconds. "Who the fuck are you?"

"I'm David, she's Ellie. Mister Thatch sent us to save your ass," he replied.

"Oh shit," Tyler muttered, looking embarrassed.

"Yeah. Stay right here, don't move, we'll be right back."

"I..." he hesitated, looking from David to Ellie, who were both, to varying degrees, failing to hide how they felt about this particular situation, and he just nodded, "Yeah, okay."

"Good."

They left the bedroom he was in and took several minutes first to clear the top floor, finding it all empty, though with several broken windows, and he was pretty sure rippers could climb, then moving down to the first story. They cleared it out, shutting the doors where they could, and returned to Tyler when they were sure they were secure.

"All right, Tyler," Ellie said, holstering her pistol and walking over to him, "mind telling us what in the *fuck* possessed you to come deep into ripper territory, alone and under-equipped?"

"I, um, I was..." he looked like he was trying to come up with a lie, and after several moments, finally gave up with a sigh, his shoulders slumping. "I was here looking for something. My girlfriend, she lives on the farm with me, she used to live here, with her family, last year. When the place got attacked and they had to run, she lost her ring. Her family ring. Her mom gave it to her, and her grandma gave it to her mom, it's been in the family for generations. I wanted to, you know, to get it back for her."

Ellie let out a loud, irritated sigh, but David felt some sympathy.

"I can't leave without it," Tyler added, some steel coming into his voice.

"You damn well–" Ellie began, taking a step towards him.

"Ellie," David said.

"What?!" she snapped, turning to look at him.

"We're at a prime location, a *new* location, and it's not like we're going to have a good opportunity to come back again. We should search it for supplies."

She stared at him a moment longer, arms crossed, tail twitching furiously, then she looked back at Tyler. "Forty five minutes, and then we're leaving, regardless."

"Thank you," he said. "I'll get started looking for it. You'll let me know if you see it?"

"Yes," David replied. "What does it look like?"

"It's just a simple gold ring."

"Get to it," Ellie said, and walked out of the room. David followed after her as she walked down the stairs.

"You're being a little harsh, don't you think?" he asked as they walked into the kitchen and started searching.

"No, he's being more than a little fucking stupid," she growled, yanking open the first of several cabinets and poking around inside. "Comes out here into *known* ripper-infested land, armed with a goddamned six-shooter, a *revolver!* Takes fucking forever to reload, fucking idiot. You're being too soft," she replied.

"Weren't you *just* telling me last night how happy you are that I'm dating Cait because I'm such a nice person?" he asked, checking the fridge.

She didn't say anything, just kept hunting fervently, occasionally yanking something from inside and slamming it down on the countertop.

"Okay, he went off half-cocked, I get it. It *was* stupid. But you've never done the same thing?" he asked.

"Oh shut up," she replied after a minute, and he laughed.

"Or what?" he asked. "What are you going to do to me, Ellie?"

She stopped what she was doing, walked over to him, and extended one finger, with a claw out, towards him. She hooked him by his belt with the claw and pulled him towards her, looking into his eyes.

"You really want to find out?"

"Well I do now," he replied.

She stared at him with her wild cat eyes for a few seconds longer, then gave him a firm kiss on the mouth. He began to kiss her back, but then she pulled back and gave him a little shove.

"You fucking tease!" he snapped as she walked away.

"Yeah, yeah, quit complaining and get back to work," she replied.

"You're lucky we aren't alone or I'd bend you the fuck over and punish the fuck out of you," David said, going back to his search.

"I'd *love* to see you try," she murmured.

"Oh really?"

"Really. You'll have to show me someday."

"I'll keep that in mind."

They performed a search of the kitchen, trying to be as thorough as they could in the time available to them. They managed to gather up a dozen cans of food, mostly vegetables, some fruits, and even some spices and seasonings that David was thrilled to slip into his pack.

They moved on to a living room, searching beneath the furniture and anywhere else anything might be hidden, all while keeping an eye out the windows. As they finished their search of the living room, which proved fruitless, and moved on to the rest of the ground floor, with him taking a small bathroom and Ellie taking a bedroom, he began to see movement.

Zombies had wandered in, no doubt drawn in by the firefight. They didn't seem particularly sure about where the fresh meat was, but they did seem sure that fresh meat was around somewhere close. David kept quiet and opened up a medicine cabinet.

He felt his heart leap as he spied, for fucking once in his life, medicine in a goddamned medicine cabinet! It was just a bottle of painkillers and a half-empty bottle of antibiotics, and a few bandages, but that was a huge find as far as he was concerned. Under the sink, he even found some cough syrup and hid it away in his pack, thinking of Ann and her sick child.

After making sure nothing else was hidden away, checking the toilet tank and finding nothing, he joined Ellie and helped her. They found some clothes and a small suitcase that they shoved full of clothes, any scraps of cloth they could find, really.

Blankets were in short supply, and a few of the people at the campgrounds were good with sewing. And David knew they could always use more clothes. Especially with winter in full bloom and the potential for more people showing up right around the corner.

Once that was done, they headed upstairs. He had been keeping his eye out for a ring but so far he hadn't seen anything like that. Ellie headed into the second story bathroom and David moved to where Tyler was.

"Any luck?" he asked.

"No, nothing yet. You?" Tyler replied.

"No ring."

"Sorry."

He just grunted and kept looking.

David left him to it, heading to another room that looked like it might once have been a study or an office. Several bookshelves were totally barren. He poked through every drawer in a desk and found nothing.

After looking under the desk and in any of the shadowy areas, he headed for the only other door in the room. Opening it up, he found a small closet that was almost totally bare. There was an old jacket inside, the only thing in sight, hanging from a hanger in the center of the closet.

There was something oddly specific about it. David turned on his flashlight, checking the shelf overhead and the floor beneath, finding nothing but dust and trash.

He reached into the pockets of the jacket, found nothing. He pulled the jacket off the hanger. It was a good jacket, at least. He hesitated as he heard something clink inside, something metal. Opening it up, he saw that there was an inner pocket.

David reached in and felt his heart skip a beat as he wrapped a fist around several pieces of metal, what felt like jewelry. He pulled out a handful and found half a dozen rings, three mismatched earrings, and a necklace with a gold chain.

"Oh fuck me," he whispered.

Moving over to the desk, he set it all down, then reached in and pulled out the rest. More earrings, another two rings, and another pair of necklaces. No, not a necklace, one of them was an old pocketwatch with a golden chain. It all looked to be in pretty good condition. David studied them. Jewelry was a curious thing in the new world.

Most people would either laugh at the notion of it, or, occasionally, they'd find something that caught their fancy and pay a little bit for it. But there were some who would go out of their way to pay shitloads of supplies and resources for even just a few pieces.

From what he understood, there were three different kinds of people who did this. The first and most common were traders who knew about the other two types of people. The second were collectors, largely people who still remembered the old world, and apparently jewelry had been a sign of wealth and status.

The third, and most rare, were those who still made technology, and needed certain rare kinds of metal to make such technology, some of which was in jewelry. So rings and earrings and necklaces were the kinds of things that could either be totally useless finds, or hugely massive windfalls that could help you for months.

David saw one of the rings that stood out, the one

that no doubt Tyler was looking for.

"Well, shit," he muttered. This put him in an awkward position.

"What?" Ellie asked, coming into the room. "Did you find something? Oh fuck," she said as she came to stand next to him. "That's...a lot."

"Yeah. Which puts us in an awkward place," he replied.

"What? No it doesn't. One of those rings is what he's looking for. We give it to him. We lay claim to everything else," Ellie said.

"Some of these might be his girlfriend's family's, not to mention, he's probably already in deep shit for doing this."

"He *should* be."

"He doesn't seem like a bad guy. I feel bad just sending him back empty-handed."

"We saved his fucking life," Ellie replied. He stared at her. "I am *not* being selfish, David!" she snapped softly. "We have an entire village of people to think about, he's got his girl and his own ass to think about. He did something stupid, he'd be fucking *lucky* to come back alive, unharmed, and with her goddamned ring."

"So you found it?"

Both of them whirled around, and Ellie seemed particularly pissed, probably because she hadn't heard him standing there in the doorway.

"Yes. You heard all that?" David asked.

"Yeah." He looked uncomfortable. "I mean, I get it, you're right. This was stupid, I was just...desperate. My girlfriend's been really fucking miserable lately and it hurts so much watching her be miserable and I thought...this would help. And, I know I have no right to ask, but...yes, I would really, *really* appreciate it if

I could bring *something* back.

"I'm going to catch goddamn hell for doing this, but if I come back with something useful, they'll be a lot less angry. I'm not completely sure about all of that, what might have belonged to her family or might not, but I do at least know that the pocketwatch was her dad's, and her mom had blue earrings..."

David looked at Ellie, who stared back at him. He waited. So did she. He remained silent, interested to hear what she had to say. Finally, she threw her arms up in frustration. "Fine! You get the ring, the earrings if they're there, the pocketwatch, and two other rings, but *nothing* else and then we are dragging your ass back home!" she snapped.

"Thank you so much," he replied.

She just marched over to the window and crossed her arms. She stood there, staring out it, tail twitching angrily. Tyler came over and he and David sorted it out. He took three of the rings and the pocketwatch, and then found the pair of earrings in question, the only blue ones among the set. He pocketed it all, then looked reluctantly at the jacket.

"Yeah?" David asked, following his gaze.

"I'm almost sure that was her mom's," he murmured.

"All right," David replied, and handed it to him after double-checking the pockets.

"Thank you for this. Really," Tyler said, accepting it.

"I'm just glad we could help. Let's get you back home," David replied. He glanced at Ellie. He thought she would've had another outburst at him giving up the jacket, it *was* a nice jacket, but she said nothing. Instead, as they began to head for the exit, she turned around sharply and marched across the room.

They left the abandoned farm in silence.

CHAPTER FIVE

"I'm sorry, Ellie," David said about a minute after they had begun walking away from the farm, payout in hand.

It was heavy and Ellie had let him carry it, as well as the suitcase. They'd packed a bag with a dozen cans of food, several cuts of beef and bacon, a loaf of bread, and a collection of a half-dozen eggs. He had two gallon glass jugs of milk in his pack.

This shit was fucking *heavy*.

They had made it back without a problem, having to kill a handful of zombies and a few more rippers that had showed up. The gate guard looked relieved to see Tyler, and gave him a lot of shit, as did William when he came out to greet and thank them. David had asked him one more time to rethink his position on offering help with the assault, but William had steadfastly, though reluctantly, turned him down, again apologizing.

And, finally, off they had gone, back home.

"It's fine," Ellie said finally. Her tail was still twitching, and it sounded like it most certainly was *not* fine.

"Are you just saying that?" David asked.

She heaved an explosive sigh. "You did a nice thing. I think it was a little questionable, you're taking a lot on faith, but ultimately it was a good move. Probably. I'm just pissed. I'm pissed that we had to waste time tracking down some idiot teenager with a hard-on who risked his, and our, lives. It's frustrating, I'm pissed, I'm getting over it. I just need time for the anger to dissolve. So, it's fine," she explained.

"Okay," David replied quietly after a moment.

He could understand that. He'd often found himself in situations where he was fucking furious, and he knew he was overreacting, but that didn't help as much as it should. So he just shut up and kept quiet until they had made their way all the way back to the campgrounds. He saw Amanda up on top of the cabin near the front, on guard duty.

"Hello, Amanda," he said.

"Hello, David," she replied with some surprising sultriness to her voice. "I see you two had a successful mission."

"Partially successfully," David replied. "I take it everything is well here?"

"Everything's perfect," she replied, smiling beautifully at him.

He just nodded and headed inside with Ellie. When they were moving Jim and Amanda's family in, Evelyn had said that Amanda was checking him out, and suggested that they might be in an open marriage.

David thought it unlikely but...a lot of unlikely things had happened. And over the past two weeks, Amanda had been surprisingly flirtatious with him. He didn't know if she intended to take it anywhere or if that's just how she was sometimes. She was certainly attractive enough, and he would *love* to have sex with her.

He'd never fucked a married woman before.

But so far, it hadn't been anything beyond suggestive glances and tones of voice, a few certain phrases that aroused his suspicions, (and his lust), and a few touches here and there. Nothing definitive. Maybe someday.

As he headed for the main office, he glanced

back one more time and saw her standing atop the roof, facing away from him. Good fucking lord her ass in those jeans. She probably had like twenty years on him, which only made him want her more.

He heard Ellie laugh softly.

"What?" he murmured.

"I see you looking."

"I mean...yeah. Who wouldn't?"

"I don't know. I know she's married, though."

"Yeah, but...okay, am I crazy or was she flirting with me?" he asked.

"She was," Ellie replied. "I've seen her do it a few times. She likes you. But I can't tell if she's just teasing you or if she's looking for something."

"Evie said she might be in an open marriage..."

"Now there's a pleasant thought."

They headed into the main office, up the stairs, and into the dining area where Evelyn and Ashley were seated at the dining table with several pieces of paper set out.

"Oh good, you're back, and apparently you brought a shitload of food," Ashley said.

"That's not the only thing we brought," David replied. He reached into his pocket and pulled out the remaining jewelry and set it on the table.

"Oh shit," Evelyn murmured.

"Jewelry? You brought jewelry?" Ashley asked, frowning.

"If I recall, when we saved your sweet ass, you were looking for jewelry," David replied as Ellie walked past them, towards the kitchen, to put up their food.

"Yeah. It meant something to me. It had personal value. Functionally speaking, it's almost useless. So..."

"There are people who would give up twenty pounds of meat for one of those rings," Evelyn said, taking one of the rings and holding it up, studying it in the sunlight.

"Are you fucking serious?" Ashley asked.

"Yeah. Collectors. Or technology-makers. It may take a few months, it make take a year, but we could make a *killing* off of these."

"Well, cool then," Ashley replied, and returned her attention to the sheets of paper.

"How are things proceeding?" David asked, setting his suitcase and backpack on the floor for the moment and sitting down at the table.

"Good. We just got finished going around and asking everyone what they're good at and what they're cool with doing. At the moment, we're establishing a guard rotation. We've got myself, Ashley, Ashley's parents, Jim, Amanda, you, Ellie, Benjamin, and Cait to work with. We're aiming for six hour shifts, which means four shifts a day, two at night right now, so that means alternating days for all of us. Four of us on one day, four of us on the next. Although it's difficult right now because you, Ellie, and Cait are running around, so I'm setting up a temporary schedule."

"We're also figuring out other schedules. The Walsh's are going to take over snow-melting duty for the next however long. Mrs. Walsh is also great at sewing, so I've put her in charge of gathering up all of our spare clothes, breaking down the useless stuff and using it to fix the messed up stuff. It'll be great to have spares, for us and to trade with.

"We're also figuring out a wood chopping schedule and game hunting schedule. Ann knows how to make snares, to trap rabbits, and she also knows how to make fish traps, for the river. It isn't *too* far from here. I figured we could set up a daily pilgrimage out to some fish traps eventually," Ashley explained.

"This is excellent," David replied. "Thank you for doing this."

"Happy to," Evelyn replied, smiling broadly. "I have a particular love of organization and lists and schedules. I'm good at it and I like doing it, honestly. So this is great."

"I'm glad. Cait left, right?" he asked.

"Yes. She woke up about ten minutes after you left, and was out the door ten minutes after that, so she should already be there and doing whatever it is," Evelyn replied.

"Okay, good. I'm going to go get this sorted."

He got up and joined Ellie in the kitchen. They spent the next ten minutes putting away the food and making sure it was well-organized and secured, so that Frostbite, or any of his friends, if they were around, wouldn't get into it.

When that was done, Ellie said she was going to throw together some vegetable beef soup for them, and he thanked her and headed upstairs to sort through the clothes and other items he'd brought back from the abandoned farmhouse.

He took a few of the clothes that he thought might fit him, (he didn't have a whole lot at this point), and ended up putting the rest in a pile to be sorted through by April, Ellie, and Cait. Though he hesitated at that.

Should they get first pick just because they were the ones 'in charge'?

The idea made him uncomfortable, and he figured it would do to determine if anyone else in the campgrounds were hurting for clothes right now. They hadn't mentioned it, but clothes might not necessarily jump to mind when you had things like food and medicine to consider. He sighed softly as he began hunting around for a place to hide the jewelry.

He was so bad with shit like this, and that just made him appreciate Evelyn all the more. She clearly excelled at keeping all sorts of stuff in her head at the same time, or at least knew enough to be able to put together charts and lists and schedules on paper to keep it all in order.

And it was only going to get more complex.

David had the idea that he was more going to be a fighter and, at best, a facilitator. Evelyn would inform him that they needed something that was dangerous to get, and he would be one of the ones to actually go out and get it.

He was happy to throw in and do the grunt work during the quieter, day-to-day moments: chopping firewood, pulling guard duty, making meals. But he got the feeling that everyone was going to have something unique to offer the community, something special, and his special thing was going to be walking out into the dangerous wilderness and procuring items or completing missions.

He never would have thought so, but he was surprisingly good at it.

Of course, right now a lot of that had to do with the fact that Ellie or Cait were with him almost all of the time, and they knew what they were doing several levels above him.

After storing the jewelry with the guns in their makeshift 'armory', which was little more than a dresser drawer, he returned to the kitchen and chatted with Ellie as she tended to the stew, stirring it occasionally.

He still felt a little awkward after their serious conversations they'd been having lately. She seemed a little more subdued than usual, maybe a little more reserved than he was used to seeing her act, and he wasn't sure if that was a good thing or a bad thing. On a whim, he walked up behind her and placed his hands on her shoulders.

"What are you doing?" she asked.

"Rubbing your shoulders...if that's okay," he replied.

"Yeah. That's fine...um, thanks," she murmured.

He began to massage her shoulders, and she immediately let out a long, satisfied sigh. "Shit," she whispered after a moment, and he felt her tail drifting slowly back and forth between his thighs, "that's really good."

"You're tense," he replied.

She laughed softly. "Yeah, you could say that."

"You should try relaxing a little more. I mean, I get it: you live a dangerous life, more so than most of us, and by choice to a certain degree, but...being by yourself all the time has to suck to a certain extent. You can relax around us."

"Why are you so interested in my life?" she asked after a few moments.

"You're my friend, Ellie. I care about you. I want you to be happy," he replied. "I...thought that was obvious, at this point." He paused. "Am I bugging you? I'm sorry, I'm not trying to pester you into doing anything. I know some people try to do that. They see something they don't like in the way someone else lives their life, and they pester and bug and nag them under the guise of 'worrying about them' or something like that. That's not what I'm trying to do. I want you to live the life you want to live, I don't want to impose on you, but I also want you to know that...friends are available to you, Ellie. Having a place you can just relax, a safe place that has people you can trust in it, is available to you. You don't have to solo every aspect of your entire life."

She was silent for several minutes after he said that, and he continued massaging her shoulders, then her neck, waiting for her to respond. Her tail had increased a little bit in its swaying, but not much, so that was good, at least.

"Thank you," she said finally. "I don't undervalue your friendship, and the things you do for me. I don't want you to think that. I just...I've learned the hard way that it's often better to live without certain...luxuries, because they can be ripped away from you at any moment. Which is more true than ever now. I appreciate what you do, and what Evie and Cait and April and Ashley do for me. I really do. I just...need to live a certain way. I don't know if that's ever going to change. I'm pretty fucked up, and I don't know if I can be fixed, but whatever happens, however I turn out...thank you. I *do* appreciate you."

"Okay," he said, and he hugged her from behind, holding her against himself. "I'm glad you're my friend, Ellie."

She laughed softly. "So am I. You're...very patient. It's more than I deserve."

"You deserve friends. And to be happy."

"Maybe someday I'll believe that," she murmured. "But for now, the soup is about to spill over."

"Oh, right. I'll get bowls," he said.

He kissed her neck, then released her and went for bowls. Finding two of them, he set them out, then went and checked to see if the others wanted anything. Ashley said no, but Evelyn was hungry, so he went and got another bowl. They served the soup, and grabbed cups of water, and then sat down to lunch.

As they ate and relayed what had happened at the abandoned farmhouse to the others, David couldn't dissuade a growing sense of discomfort. Cait should probably be back by now, given how long they had been gone. It wasn't *that* far of a walk over to the doctor's...

"What's wrong?" Ellie asked.

David realized that he'd fallen silent after finishing his stew. "Nothing," he replied. Ellie stared at him. He sighed. "Is it that obvious?"

"Yes. What's wrong?" she replied.

"I'm just worried about Cait. I don't know why. I guess I feel like she should be back by now..."

"She *did* also have to track down Jennifer," Evelyn pointed out.

"Yeah...I dunno, I just feel a little weird about it."

"Hmm." Ellie frowned, looking down at the table for a moment. Then she looked back up, met his eyes. "If it'll make you feel better, we can go to the doctor's outpost and see what's happening for ourselves. At worst, we'll run into Cait on her way back."

He nodded. "Yeah, okay. If you don't mind."

She stood. "I don't mind." She hesitated, looking down at the meal. "Uh, would you mind..."

"You made lunch, I'll clean it up," Evelyn replied with a kind smile. "Go."

"Thanks."

David gave Evelyn and Ashley kisses, then went

to grab his gear and head out with Ellie.

...

"You think she's okay?" David asked as they approached the bridge that would take them over the river.

"Cait's a big girl, she can take care of herself almost as well as I can," Ellie replied, but he thought he detected a little note of worry in her voice. Another moment went by before she spoke up again. "How do you do it?" she asked.

"Do what?" he replied.

"Maintain a relationship with three women. Two of them different species. I mean, I've never found it particularly hard to relate to someone based on their species...unless it was a human. No offense, but in my experience, it seems like inhumans see seven different species across the land, and humans see...well, humans and not-humans. They lump everyone not like them into one category, if that makes sense...again, no offense..."

"No, I get it. I mean, I've seen that, too. I know what you're talking about. If anything, I've found that I relate to inhumans more than humans. Which I guess makes it sound a little along the lines of what you just said, but I don't see everyone that way. I've learned to be far more concerned with what people do, versus what they are, you know?"

"Yeah, me too."

"As for how I do it? I don't fucking know. I still feel like I'm stumbling through every day. I don't know if I'm doing a great job or a terrible job. I'm just...trying to make everyone happy, and take care of them, and engage with them."

"And fuck them," she murmured.

"That too, obviously. They are all...*really* horny. Especially Cait. Good fucking God I've never met such a sexually needy woman. Not that I'm complaining."

"Oh I know you're just in lust with Cait, I mean, who isn't? She's the most attractive woman I've ever seen, and I think most people would agree with that."

"She's...something else. I don't know what she sees in me or why she felt the need to go forward with a relationship..."

"Well, I don't know why she felt the need to jump the gun there either. I actually asked her about that..." she hesitated.

"And?" he asked.

"I need to stop telling you this stuff," she murmured.

"Too late now, Ellie. Spill it," David replied.

She laughed. "Okay, but only because I don't think the answer will cause problems. She admitted she didn't know, she just liked you *so* much, and felt compelled to be a part of your life. Personally, I think she's lonelier than she'll admit to anyone, even herself. Especially herself. Only she didn't really realize how lonely she was until she met you. But as for what she saw in you? I mean, it's obvious. You're kind, you're patient, you're honest and trustworthy and you know how to communicate and you're *really* good at eating pussy."

"I guess that makes sense," he replied.

"You're a good guy, David. Don't...let how I've handled our friendship, you know, make you think less of yourself. *Please* don't do that," she said.

"Oh, don't worry about that, Ellie. I've been questioning and depreciating myself *long* before you arrived on the scene," he replied.

She laughed. "Well...good to know."

Up ahead, he finally saw the bridge they were to cross. He opened his mouth to say something else, but froze and clammed up as he saw something up by the bridge. From the way Ellie stiffened and froze as well, he figured she had seen it too.

"What is that?" he whispered finally, his hand resting on the butt of his pistol. He'd opted out of taking his SMG again, partially because he'd chewed through a lot of ammo, but also because he'd been a little paranoid in the other direction before leaving, thinking that maybe something might happen at home, and now he wondered if he'd regret that. *Something* was slinking along the ground near the bridge in an entirely disturbing and creepy fashion.

"I don't...know," Ellie whispered. "I think–"

Whatever it was, it stopped abruptly and suddenly shot upright, standing on two legs. It was sleek and grayish and had a somewhat bulbous head. Its silhouette struck fear, powerful and freezing fear, into his heart.

It twisted around to face them suddenly. Its face was a visage of pure terror. It had two huge black eyes and a circular mouth stuffed full of teeth. Those huge eyes came to rest on the pair of them, and it issued a piercing shriek.

Both David and Ellie cried out as half a dozen other bulbous heads suddenly appeared from around their surroundings, and they shot to their feet and began coming right towards them, the seven monsters rushing towards them in a frenzied manic stampede.

"Vipers!" Ellie screamed suddenly, and opened fire.

David ripped his pistol from its holster, took aim,

and opened fire. His first few shots went wild, but he forced himself to get a fucking grip, aimed at one of those big, round heads that was running straight for him, and squeezed the trigger.

The shot connected and the thing lost its footing, going down like a puppet with its strings cut. It flopped on the ground a few times before going still, and something about that turned his stomach. He shifted aim and fired again, managing to catch another one in its big, ugly head and punching a hole through it. Dark gray blood flew on the air as its brains were ejected from its body, and it flopped to the ground, too.

They kept on firing, frantically trying to put the creatures down before they got a chance to reach them, get in close, and do some real damage. He fired every shot he had and finally managed to bring a third one down after shooting it twice in the chest and once in the neck. Ellie was at least more precise with her shots, but he could tell she was a bit shaken as well.

"Holy *fuck!*" she hissed after a few seconds.

"*These* are *vipers!?*" David replied, his voice harsh but quiet. He had heard of vipers, but as far as he knew he'd never actually seen one in the flesh.

And he was deeply grateful for that fact, because these things were fucking horrifying.

"Yeah," Ellie murmured, reloading her pistol. He shakily did the same thing. "Squids that have been turned by the virus," she whispered. "Haven't seen any of those for months and months now. Fucking hell, I *hate* these damned things. Something's wrong, though."

"What?" he asked.

"They shouldn't be this far inland. We're a good two miles from the lake. If they came this far up the river, either it's a fluke or...something's very wrong."

"Like what?"

"I don't know. But come on, we should hurry."

They set off towards the bridge, keeping a wary eye out for more vipers.

CHAPTER SIX

David felt relief tentatively begin to edge in as he caught sight of the doctor's outpost, the building that they had converted into both hospital and home. Although it was a relatively short walk once they got across the bridge, it still seemed to take forever.

But now they were on approach. He just prayed that everyone was actually okay. He and Ellie jogged up to the front door and skidded to a halt as someone appeared in the window overhead.

"That's close enough-oh, hi, Ellie," a woman said.

"Hi, Katya. Everything okay here?" Ellie replied.

David found himself staring up at a brutally attractive woman with a scar down one side of her face and short brown hair.

"Not exactly," she muttered, sounding annoyed.

"What's wrong?" Ellie asked, alarmed.

"Oh, I mean, nothing immediately dangerous. Come inside." She paused, looked at David. "Hmm. You must be the David I've heard so much about."

"Uh...from who?"

"First Jennifer. Now Cait. I'll let you in." She disappeared.

"You're popular," Ellie murmured as they approached the front door.

"Apparently," he replied.

A moment later, the door opened up, though it wasn't Katya who opened it, but a familiar face.

"Jennifer!" David said, happily surprised.

"Hi, David," she replied with a small smile.

He opened his arms. "Hug?"

She nodded and stepped forward, hugging him.

He hadn't seen her since they'd parted ways the night after they'd slept together for the first time, though not intentionally. He would have seen her gladly if he'd had the time.

"How have you been?" he asked as he held her to him.

"Busy," she replied. "When I wasn't snowed in. You?"

"Same."

She pulled back slightly and stared at him with her bloodshot, gray eyes. "I've missed you," she said, and then she kissed him on the mouth.

"I've missed you, too," he replied when the kiss ended. "A lot."

"Yeah, I imagine so after what happened last time you two spent some time together," Ellie said with a smirk.

"Hush!" Jennifer snapped at her.

He studied her. She was just as beautiful as he remembered: a little taller than average for a human woman, thin and trimly built, her skin as pale as snow, shot through with dark veins. Her black hair was chin-length, down, framing her beautiful face. She was a wraith, the only wraith he had ever really known.

Certainly the only wraith he had ever had sex with.

"Yeah...I guess I can see it."

He looked over and spied Katya, standing in the doorway, leaning against the frame, hands clasped together in front of her. She was smirking.

"See what?" he asked.

"The appeal. There must be appeal if Cait *and* Jennifer are fucking you. And Ellie, from what I hear," she said, her smirk broadening.

"Shut up, Katya," Ellie replied.

"Oh yeah, you're definitely riding his cock."

"Eat me, bitch," Ellie growled, flipping her off.

"Been a while," Katya replied with a shrug.

"Where's Cait?" David asked, looking around the room. He only saw a few of the people who lived there, he couldn't remember their names, but he remembered their faces at least.

"She's through here," Katya said.

"Is she okay?" Ellie asked.

"Yeah, she's fine. Why are you so worried?" Katya replied.

"We ran into a pack of vipers on the way here. They came from the river, at the bridge."

Katya stiffened. "Vipers? All the way up here?"

"Fuck, that might explain what happened," one of the others in the room, a stern-faced, red-furred jag that he recognized from before, said. Her name started with a J, he was almost certain.

"What happened?" Ellie asked as David began heading for the door.

"We're running low on a particularly unique supply..." the jag began to explain, and David left them to it for now, wanting to check on Cait. He stepped past Katya and into another room with a row of narrow beds and several tables that had a lot of medical supplies set up across them. This was likely their main infirmary. Cait and the man he recognized from before, the one who headed up the group, with graying brown hair and glasses, Donald, were standing across the room. He was talking quietly to her, and she was staring at him, seated on one of the beds.

She looked...

He wasn't sure what her expression conveyed, if

it was good or bad.

Then she saw him and her eyes lit up and she jumped to her feet. "David!"

"Hi, Cait. Is everything okay?" he asked.

"Um..." she glanced at Donald. "Yes, just fine." She whispered something to him, and he glanced at David, then nodded and put on an awkward smile, then she crossed the room quickly and wrapped him in a hug. "Hi! Are *you* okay? Why are you here?" she asked. "Not that I'm unhappy, I just...thought you and Ellie were going to wait for me."

"We were. We got worried," he replied, hugging her back.

"I'm okay. And Jennifer's here already! And, uh, they need our help," she said.

"I heard some of it in the main room..." David replied.

"Yes, please, let's all go to the main room and discuss this. We could very much use your help again, I'm sorry to say. Not that we don't appreciate the help! I just wish that we had fewer problems, or that we were more capable of handling them on our own..." Donald said.

"It's fine," Cait replied. "We can help. Come on."

She led the two of them back into the main room, where Ellie, Katya, the jag medic, and a goliath woman were gathered. The goliath woman was as intimidating as she was attractive. She looked a bit older, maybe in her late thirties, and had short hair so blonde it was almost white. Her eyes were a frigid blue and shone in her pale face, making her look almost ghostly.

She was a bit taller than Evelyn, and well-built. She looked like she could lift a truck. She leaned against a wall with her arms across her chest, wearing a dirty hoodie, cargo pants, and big, black boots. She looked at David with an appraising, if intimidating, gaze, and smirked just a little as he looked back at her. She must be the other person who provided security, he surmised.

"Okay, okay," Donald said as they came in. "Let's, uh, let's talk about this. I'm not sure if you've met the rest of our team. They were absent when last you were here. This is Katya, our, um..." he hesitated.

"Combat medic, doc. Told you that already. I'm a combat medic," Katya said.

"Yes, I know, I just...with Lima Company in the region and how tense things are with them, I worry about possible connections people might draw between that phrase and them..." Donald replied uncertainly.

"I've never been with Lima Company," Katya said, looking at David. "I was a soldier for ten years. Basically, I put people back together under fire."

"Wow. You must be extremely skilled and brave," he replied.

"I am."

"Indeed. This is Vanessa. She's our...security expert," Donald said, looking at the goliath.

"More or less," Vanessa said. She had a somewhat deeper, but very smooth voice. "I fuck people up when they fuck with us. Among other things."

"Yes...quite," Donald murmured. "Anyway. Our, ah, issue. One of our most precious resources is blood. We keep spare blood chilled, on site, so that we can give a transfusion if it becomes necessary. Typically, if it is necessary, time is a factor. That was largely what you were helping us maintain when you were here last. Now, as to our current predicament, it's not exactly an *emergency* per se, but I feel it does dovetail nicely with what Cait has been telling us so far. Typically speaking, when it comes to giving blood, there are different types of blood.

"Type A, Type B, Type AB, so on. Usually, you must match these types between donor and recipient. Which makes it more complicated. However, there is one blood type that can be put into anyone: Type O Negative. While that made it useful before, it is far more useful now, as that remains true even across the human-inhuman spectrum. Anyone, be they goliath or jag or even nymph or squid can safely receive Type O Negative blood. This makes it valuable. To complicate matters, it is rare. Or, at least, around here it is." He hesitated as, somewhere far off, they heard a gunshot echo across the land.

They all waited, tensing. Nothing else happened.

With a soft sigh, Donald continued. "We have found exactly one person with this blood type, and so far he has been rather accommodating, agreeing to donate once every two months."

"That seems...less often than you'd think," Cait murmured.

"There are health risks associated with donating more often than that, and even that often makes me nervous. The point is, we're out, and he was due here two days ago. We haven't heard anything from him, and we were going to investigate, only we've had increasing difficulty with stalkers. One got into the building yesterday..."

"Shit, that's terrifying," David muttered.

"Yes. We were lucky," Donald replied. "This man in question, Elias, lives in the fishing village at the edge of Indigo Lake."

"Yeah, and we think we might know what it could be now," Katya said unhappily.

"What?" Donald asked.

"We ran into a pack of vipers at the bridge on the way here," Ellie told him.

"Oh dear. That's...very problematic," he muttered, looking down slowly at the pitted and scarred wooden floor in concentration. "This region seems to be growing more dangerous."

"Something we're hoping to fix," Ellie said.

"Oh yes. Cait mentioned that you were going after the thieves that have been harassing us all over the past few months," he replied, looking back up.

"And we wanted help. I want Vanessa and Katya to help with the assault," Ellie said.

"I'm sorry, that's out of the question," Donald replied immediately. "As it is, I'm reluctant to even dispatch one of them, as much as I agree with your cause and hope it succeeds."

David sighed softly, but noticed Ellie looking intently at Katya and Vanessa. She raised her eyebrows. Neither of them looked necessarily like they were on the same page as Donald. Finally, Vanessa spoke up.

"As much as Donald has an overabundance of worry and anxiety about every little thing...he's not wrong this time. The stalkers are becoming a real problem. But listen, Ellie, deal with this problem for us, I promise I'll be there with my big gun and a hearty desire to kick ass."

"Why do *you* get to go?" Katya asked petulantly.

"Because I've got seniority here. I'm pulling rank," Vanessa replied in a tone that brooked no argument.

Katya just sighed and crossed her arms.

"So it's settled then? We find this Elias, get him to donate blood, and you'll help us attack the thieves?" he asked.

Vanessa nodded. They looked at Donald. He sighed softly. "Yes, we have a deal."

"Okay, then. We'll be back just as soon as we figure out what's up with this guy," Ellie said. She turned and began walking towards the exit.

"Can I come with you?" Jennifer asked.

David glanced at her, then at Ellie, then at Cait. Cait still looked distracted. What was going on with her?

"We could use the help," Ellie said. "You remember how to shoot, right?"

Jennifer rolled her eyes. "Give me a fucking break, Ellie."

"All right then, let's get a move on. Sooner we can do this, the better."

"We'll be back as soon as we can," David said as they headed for the exit.

"Good luck," Donald replied.

They all walked back out into the frigid air.

. . .

There was another path through the forest, an old dirt road that was still decently well-maintained, that led them west, away from the hospital. As the four of them struck off, David found himself torn between catching up with Jennifer and wondering what was up with Cait. Because something was. She'd hardly said anything, and she was staring ahead of them, her face a flat, neutral expression.

Had she just gotten some awful news? Was something wrong with her?

Ultimately, he decided that whatever it was, she would probably tell him in due time. So he allowed himself to be distracted by Jennifer, who was really distracting right now. She walked very close beside him, and quickly took his hand in hers. As soon as she did, however, she let go and looked over at him nervously.

"Sorry, I should ask. Are we like...are we good?" she asked.

"What? Yeah, of course," he replied, offering his hand. A look of powerful relief swept across her face and she smiled broadly as she took his hand. It was interesting to see her being so...expressive. Good, but interesting.

"Sorry. I didn't know where we actually, uh, were. With how we...feel about each other. I mean, I know how *I* feel, obviously, it's just that I wasn't really sure how you felt about me, or us, or touching, since we haven't had a chance to see each other since then. Not that I'm mad! I mean, I get it, you must have been busy..."

"Jennifer, oh my God, you're fucking babbling," Ellie said.

"Piss off!" Jennifer shot back.

"Am I wrong?"

"Jennifer," David said, trying to mediate, "I'm happy to see you, I still feel very good about what happened between us, and yes, I was very, very busy, and I'm sorry I didn't get a chance to see you. I would have gladly taken it."

"...okay," she said, and stepped closer to him as they walked.

He let go of her hand and slipped an arm around her slim waist, and she pressed herself against him. "So, I don't want to put a stop to it, but you seem very...exuberant. Compared to the first time we met," David said.

"Oh. Yeah. Well, let's just say you kind of opened up Pandora's Box–"

"*Yeah,* he did," Ellie muttered, smirking.

"Fuck *off,* Ellie! Anyway. I've had a lot of reason to be cautious and anxious and not trust people, and it has caused me to become very, shall we say, reserved. And I wasn't really naturally like that, before...I became a wraith. And you've awoken my natural...exuberance."

"Is *that* what you call it when you're horny?" Ellie asked.

"You are such a sassy fucking *bitch* today, aren't you?" Jennifer snapped.

"Yeah. Apparently David's got me riled up too, you fucker," she said, glaring briefly at him, though she had a small smile on.

"What'd you do to her?" Jennifer asked.

"I made her be decent to someone. Twice. In a single day."

"In a single *morning,* fucker," she growled.

"Wow. I'm surprised you're still alive," Jennifer murmured.

"Now *you* shut the fuck up," Ellie said.

"What have you been doing, Jennifer?" David asked, attempting to once again get the conversation back on track. He swore that between Ellie, Cait, and now apparently Jennifer, they could bicker for hours.

"Helping the doctors," she said. "There's a lot of stuff that needs maintenance and fixing around their outpost, and they have a surprisingly healthy supply of lube, and–" She hesitated.

"And...?" David prompted.

"I've begun seeing Vanessa," she whispered.

"You *what?!*" Ellie cried.

"I shouldn't have said that," Jennifer groaned.

"Wait, what's happening? I missed that. Sorry. What's going on?" Cait asked.

"So kind of you to join us," Ellie said.

"Piss off," Cait replied, but she still sounded a little dazed. "What'd I miss?"

"Jennifer's hooking up with Vanessa," Ellie replied.

"Oh *shit*, I *knew* it. I saw the way you were looking at her. I thought you just had a crush. How serious is it?" Cait asked.

"It's not *serious*. It's just...fun. Play. We're playing. She's got this strap-on and...I've said too much. *Please* don't mention that to anyone. I don't think she'd care and I'm pretty sure everyone at the hospital already knows, I get...noisy...but still. Please?"

"We won't say anything," David replied.

"Thank you...but yeah, that's what I've been doing." She paused for a few seconds, then looked at David. "Do you think...I mean, if we have time, you'd be willing to...what I mean is, uh, David, could we...make love?"

"Yes," he replied immediately. "Enthusiastically yes."

"Oh good," Jennifer said, looking deeply relieved. "I was really hoping that was the case. I really miss you and your cock."

"I miss you and your pussy," he replied, and he kissed her. She kissed him back immediately, though stopped when he nearly tripped.

"So, um, Cait...is everything okay?" he asked after another moment.

"What? Yeah. I'm fine," she replied.

"Are you sure? You seem...distracted."

She was silent for a few seconds, not looking at him, focusing on the path ahead. "I'm okay," she replied finally.

"*Super* convincing," Ellie said.

Cait let out an exasperated sigh. "Oh my God, Ellie, I'm *fine*. Don't worry David," she said, and she seemed to really come back to herself, to the conversation, regaining her natural confidence and ease. "I'm really okay. Did you really fight vipers on the way over here?"

"We really did," Ellie replied.

"They scared the fucking shit out of me," David muttered.

"They *are* really scary," Jennifer said. "God, I hope nothing's happened. I mean, I've heard that there are vipers in and around the lake, but they're supposed to be pretty rare. I also hear that there's a group of squids living there, and sometimes they trade with the humans."

"Here's hoping nothing went wrong," Cait murmured.

They kept walking through the forest, between stands of tall, dead trees that seemed to reach towards the cloudless blue skies with skeletal fingers. The path they walked was mostly slush now as the sun warmed and melted the heavy layer of snow.

David found himself yearning for longer days and warmth and greenery again. Spring was probably his favorite time of year. It was so beautiful and it wiped away the cold, dead misery of winter. They walked along the slushy pathway for another five or so minutes before coming to a break in the trees and a fork in the road.

And, evidently, the lake. It had been too long

since he'd seen a large body of water.

The lake was quite large.

The waters were a grayish blue and mostly flat. The lake's edge, a muddy and rocky coastline, stretched away from them to either side for quite a ways, eventually curving back in on itself after several hundred meters in either direction. To his left, he could see the river and the inlet where it let into the lake, a collection of small structures, probably no more than some shacks, and further beyond those, larger structures, off in the distance.

And, not far from it, an island. All of this was edged by a forest where it wasn't by water. To the right, more structures, these closer, and he'd guess this was the fishing village. From his vantage point, granted to him by a rise in the land, he could see some wood docks extending into the water, a large, blocky structure, and a seemingly random collection of other buildings around it.

"That's it," Ellie said, facing to the right. "Come on, let's go."

"I don't see any activity," Cait murmured as they started walking.

"Neither do I. Have your guns ready," Ellie replied.

Now David was really regretting leaving his SMG behind. He should have just stuck with the fucking thing. But he had his pistol, it had some decent stopping power and he was a good shot, and he had five magazines to spare.

That was enough…

Right?

He supposed he'd find out. And he was with three other people, all of which were armed, two of which were fantastic fighters, (he wasn't sure about

Jennifer, though Ellie said she wasn't great), so he'd probably be okay.

As they approached, David got a better idea of the layout. There were about a dozen and a half ramshackle structures cobbled together from sheet metal and wood and evidently anything else the builders could get their hands on, built roughly along either side of a road that led off the main street they were now walking along to the docks themselves.

Dominating the area, in between the end of the makeshift structures and the water's edge, was an enormous metal structure that looked like the warehouse Ellie had saved his life in, and a two-story wooden structure that might once have served as a control area for the docks.

He also saw that something was definitely wrong. It was unnaturally quiet, save for the soft murmur of the lake and the occasional call of a bird or other animal. And he thought he saw still forms, dead bodies, strewn across the main road.

As they came to the junction and began making their way down the path, he confirmed that yes, that's what they were. There were a dozen corpses strewn across the area, but most of them were, he saw with a sinking feeling in his stomach, vipers. There was a lot of blood.

"Oh fuck me," Cait whispered as she saw the massacre.

"Jesus, they were hit hard," Jennifer muttered.

"We need to look for survivors," David said. He looked to Ellie, who was scowling fiercely, her eyes darting between structures, pistol in hand. "Ellie!" he hissed.

"I know!" she snapped softly. "Jennifer, with me. We'll take the left side. David, Cait, hit the right.

We'll work our way down to the warehouse. Be fucking *careful,* okay?"

"We will," Cait said. "Come on, David."

She set off, her shotgun in hand now. David followed after her. His pistol felt heavy in his hands, but reassuring. The place was a wreck. Clearly, whatever had happened here had been very bad. Many windows were broken out, and blood and bullet holes scarred the fronts of most of the buildings.

One of them had apparently burned down to the foundation, but luckily it hadn't been like River View, it hadn't spread to the surrounding structures. They approached the first building, a small shack, and Cait gently pushed the front door open.

"Is anyone here? We're here to help," she asked, raising her voice just loud enough to be heard. They waited. Nothing. "Fuck," she muttered.

She rejoined him and moved onto the next structure. Glancing across the way, he saw Ellie and Jennifer roughly doing the same, with Ellie checking the structures and Jennifer watching her back. She glanced his way and caught his eyes, a look of anxiety plain on her face. He turned his attention back to Cait, listening closely for signs of life.

They made slow, arduous progress down the fishing village. Most of the buildings were thankfully vacant of bodies. When he'd seen the state of the main road, he'd been worried that it would be a slaughterhouse, and who knew? Maybe the slaughterhouse was yet to come.

He found his eyes drawn repeatedly to the looming gray warehouse.

They continued working their way slowly down the string of buildings, occasionally turning up a dead body. The only real upside of that was that usually it was a dead viper and not a dead person. Ten long minutes passed in the cold light of day and they didn't find a single survivor.

As they came to stand between the warehouse and two-story structure, David felt the unseen presence of watching eyes. He looked around again and again, trying to see if there were any vipers lurking. For originating in the water, they seemed surprisingly adept at hiding and fighting on land. But he could see nothing, save for the corpses.

"Now what?" Jennifer asked.

"Let's search the wooden building," Ellie replied. "Then, if we don't find anyone there, we'll search the fucking warehouse."

They crossed to the wooden building, where the front door hung open. As they began to head inside, Ellie, who was leading them, froze. She whirled around and he saw her eyes go wide. David twisted around, raising his pistol.

"Oh no," he whispered.

A dozen bulbous heads were lined up next to the warehouse now, staring with huge black eyes at the four of them in total silence. Cait and Jennifer turned around as well, and both raised their weapons. One of the creatures suddenly let out a piercing shriek.

Another shriek rang out from their left, and he jerked in that direction, and saw another dozen of the horrible things lined up on the docks now.

Where were they coming from!?

All at once, the packs of vipers began sprinting towards them.

CHAPTER SEVEN

They opened fire.

All hell broke loose.

David focused his aim on one of the ones charging at him from beside the warehouse and blew its head half off, a good chunk of its brains splattering the others in a horrendous spray of gray gore. He could hear nothing but the roar of gunfire as Ellie and Jennifer opened up with their pistols, Cait with her shotgun.

She blew holes in their ranks as they drew in closer, blasting off both of her barrels before hastily cracking the weapon open and shoving two more shells in. David kept up the rate of fire. There were certainly more than enough targets to shoot at.

More of them were coming from the village now.

Had they been hiding?! He supposed it was entirely likely. There were trees and rocks and lots of bushes surrounding the little village by the lake. He tried to keep his hands steady as the hideous, alien things ran shrieking towards them, circular mouths open and hungry and desperate for fresh meat.

He dropped one, another, three in total, and wounded a few more, before his pistol ran dry. Hastily, he ejected the magazine, tore another from his pocket, and slammed it in. Then he kept aiming and firing, squeezing the trigger again and again.

Before he knew it, the second magazine was gone and this time half a dozen of the oddly wet, gray things had gone down. But there were more coming. Gunsmoke filled the frigid air as he reloaded a second time.

Suddenly, he wondered if he had enough ammo.

It didn't seem like it. Their initial numbers had not just doubled but *tripled* in the span of scarcely thirty seconds. Where the actual *fuck* where they all coming from!?

He shot another one in its weirdly round mouth and the back of its head burst open as it flopped to the ground, tripping up two more. He shifted aim and blasted another through the neck, fired again and put around round into its chest. It dropped like a ragdoll. Beside him, Ellie and Cait were screaming like Valkyries on the battlefield.

More of the awful things came at them, and how many more was this drawing in like flies to shit!? Zombies, stalkers, anything could be nearby. Sometimes they stayed away from each other, something about territory, he'd guess, but zombies mixed with pretty much every undead type from what he'd seen.

By the time he was reaching for his second to last magazine, David saw that they'd put down probably thirty of the creatures, but twice that number had arrived and were swarming in from every side. He flashed back to the time with the stalkers, and how many of them there had been. The only way they'd gotten out of that was–

He heard a shout from off to the right, back from the way they had initially come, and a glance thrown in that direction showed him several more figures rushing down the road towards them. He felt a fresh spike of terror as his initial impression was that more monsters were coming at them, but he quickly realized that their strides were too consistent, too purposeful. Not zombies or any other type of undead, reinforcements!

"Keep fighting!" he snapped, firing off more

bullets into the gray, dark-eyed creatures as they ran towards them.

Gunfire erupted as the newcomers opened fire, and immediately the vipers began wilting and dying under the concentration of incoming lead. He and the others fell back a bit towards the wooden structure, to get out of the line of fire, and after another thirty seconds or so, they had managed to put down the last of the monsters.

For several moments, no one spoke. David and his group looked at the ones who had saved them. He could immediately tell that at least they weren't from Lima Company, though that might have actually worked out for the best this time, given his need to speak with them. For a few seconds, he worried that these people might belong to the thieves, but after studying them for a bit longer, something told him no.

If he had to guess, he'd say they were the fishers who lived here.

There were about a dozen of them, all of them armed, mostly with pistols. They walked down the length of the road until they came to stand across from the four of them, and David wondered if this might turn sour. He prayed not, but he suddenly realized how this might look. They could easily be opportunistic scavengers raiding these people's homes. They weren't, but the truth didn't always matter to everyone.

"Who the fuck are you?!" someone demanded.

"Emmett, you relax, now. This is Cait and Ellie, we know them," an older man near the front said. David studied him. He reminded him of William Thatch, not in appearance, but in how he carried himself, and his presence. He was a heavyset man with scraggly blonde hair and a set of scars across his neck. He carried a long-barreled shotgun with a distinct ease, and had a pair of pistols, one on each hip. He looked very calm.

"Doesn't mean they weren't fucking robbing us–" the same voice groused.

"Emmett, don't make me regret bringing you along," the older man said. His tone shifted very, very slightly, but the effect was immediate, and the younger man who had spoken instantly clammed up.

Behind him, David felt Jennifer press against him, and he suddenly felt cold. Was it a good idea that she had come along? He had been so pleased to see her and so distracted by Cait and by the vipers they'd run into that he hadn't really thought about the implications of it. Wraiths...were a wildcard, in the reactions they provoked.

Ellie and Cait hadn't said anything, so he figured they'd know if anyone here would have a genuine problem, given how much they knew about the region and the people in it, but maybe they were just as distracted as he.

Certainly Cait was.

"Not that I don't appreciate the assistance, or am unhappy to see you, but I am curious: what are you and your friends doing here?" the elder man asked.

"We're here on behalf of the doctors...and to ask for your help with something extremely important, Murray. Can we speak with you alone?" Ellie replied, stepping forward.

"The doctors? Oh! Yes. Elias. Don't worry, he's safe. He's back with the others for now. All right, I'll talk. Split up, people, make sure we're safe! Check your homes!" he yelled.

The group reluctantly spread apart, scattering across the fishing village, and Murray walked over to them. "So, as decent as the two of you have been to the people of this village, I *do* have to ask, because they would complain to me if I didn't: you didn't take anything, right?"

"No, Murray. We didn't steal from your fucking homes," Ellie replied.

"Okay. Again, sorry, but I had to ask."

"What happened here?" Cait asked.

He sighed and looked back at the village for a moment. "Day before yesterday, it was just like most other days, and then these fuckers," he growled, glowering at the nearest viper corpse, "came boiling up out of the lake by the dozens. No warning. Nothing. We lost several people, it happened so fast, we ran.

"We first tried to get down to our secondary site, the fishing cabins down the way, but they were being attacked, too. So we gathered those who were there and fled into the forest. We ended up hiding in the abandoned town at the crossroads, but we've had several stalker and zombie attacks, and some raiders attacked this morning..."

He sighed heavily and shook his head. "We decided we had to come here and retake the village now, not later."

"Shit," Ellie muttered. "We ran into some vipers about two miles inland. I *knew* something was going wrong. But what? Why are there so many?"

"No fucking clue," Murray growled. "And it's not like we have another place to live...so why are you here?"

"Those raiders who attacked you, I'm guessing they're part of the same group that burned down River View and have been harassing the region for the past few months."

"Yeah, that makes sense," Murray replied, nodding.

"We're going after them."

"Are you now?" he murmured.

"Yes. We need help. What we want is someone to help with the assault, and I'd like to keep this quiet. No idea if they have any contacts or people in anyone's group," Ellie replied.

Murray frowned, studied them for a moment, scratched his chin and looked back out over his village and his people again, then he sighed and looked back. "I'll make you a deal," he said. "You retake the little village down the way, make it safe, and also escort Elias to the doctor's to see that our deal remains unbroken, and I'll give you someone to help out. One of the boys—"

Ellie cut him off. "No. I want Ruby."

"Ruby, huh?" he muttered. "Yeah, I was worried you might say that." He stared at her for a moment, his face becoming flat, unreadable, and she stared right back. Finally, he relented. "All right, all right, fine. I'll give you Ruby and her rifle. But *only* if you do the jobs."

"Fine. We'll need more ammo. We burned through a *lot* of bullets fighting here."

He sighed again, more heavily. "Of course you did. Fine. Come on."

He led them into the wooden building and had them wait in the entrance lobby, then he walked up across to a set of stairs and disappeared up them.

"Are you okay?" David asked, looking at Jennifer, who had stuck close to him, practically clinging to him.

"Yeah. Just...I'd actually gotten *comfortable* being around the doctors. Everyone there is, well, at least not an asshole, some are really nice to me, I just...had forgotten. How people react, you know? Some of them were staring at me like they wanted to shoot me..."

"I would never let them do that, Jennifer," Ellie said, reaching out and laying a hand gently against the side of her head. "Never."

"Thank you," she murmured. David turned around and gave her a hug, and she hugged him back tightly.

"What kind of ammo do you need?!" Murray called down.

They conferred among each other for a moment, and then Ellie shouted back, "Nine millimeters and ten gauge shells!"

"All right!"

They heard him moving around upstairs. David looked outside, at the people moving through their village. He felt for them, genuinely, but he did notice more than one of them staring back at him occasionally with dark, distrusting gazes.

He tried to ignore them. This didn't exactly feel like a nice place, but under the circumstances, he couldn't really blame them. Something about Murray felt shifty though. Maybe that was just how he was.

A few moments later, Murray returned with a small box held in both hands. He had a look that was somehow both grateful and sour.

"Look like you just bit down on a lemon," Cait said as he came over.

He sighed, exasperated. "Not you guys. I actually wanted to thank you for doing this. Just thinking about the others we asked for help. Those military dicks up the way. Sent a runner off as soon as this happened. They told us to fuck ourselves, basically.

Got something more important to do than help our sorry asses."

Ellie shot David an angry glance, but he just looked back at her. Unless he heard that they were actively shooting people on sight just for approaching, he intended to ask them for help. If you never asked, the answer was *always* no. But if you did ask, the answer just *might* be no. It made sense to ask, in this case at least.

Murray set the box down. "All I can spare."

"Thanks," Ellie replied.

They split up the ammo. David managed to get his hands on two more magazines for his pistol. Not as much as he would have liked, but better than nothing, at least. He made a mental note to start traveling with more of an arsenal on him. It would be more of a pain in the ass to carry around, but he could certainly afford to have more bullets on him, especially if he was going to be running into situations like this more often than not.

"All right," Ellie said after making sure everyone was good to go, "let's get this motherfucking show on the road."

...

"Can we have sex tonight?" Jennifer asked.

They were about back at the fork in the road they'd emerged from the woods in, marking the halfway point between the fishing village and its smaller sister site. So far, they hadn't said much of anything as they'd been making their trek.

"I thought you already asked that, but yes, definitely," he replied. "You gonna come back to the campgrounds with us?"

"Yes," she said. "I've been wanting to see them, and to meet the others I've heard about. I talked a little about it with Cait...you're *also* dating a rep *and* a goliath...is that right?" she asked.

He chuckled. "Yes, that's right. A shy rep woman named April and a goliath woman named Evelyn."

"And Cait?" she asked.

"Yep," Cait and David said at the same time.

"Wow..." she looked at Ellie. "Are *you two* dating?"

"I'm not dating anyone," Ellie replied. "I have friends that I fuck sometimes."

"Okay. Sorry, I had to ask, so much seems to have changed over the past month. And there are other people living there?" Jennifer asked.

"Yes. We have four...I guess families is accurate. What is a family anyway? Four families living there right now. I think they're all refugees from River View, like myself, Evie, and April were," David replied.

"He's also fucking this blonde girl named Ashley," Ellie murmured.

"Right! Ashley! Shit..." Cait whispered, looking alarmed.

"What? What's wrong?" David asked.

"Hmm? Uh...nothing's wrong. I just...forgot something," Cait replied.

"What'd you forget?" Ellie asked.

"I just need to talk with Ashley about something."

"Which is...?" David asked.

"Personal," Cait replied after a moment.

He looked over at her, then at Ellie, who also looked confused.

"Why is everything personal and private all of a sudden?" Ellie asked.

"It isn't," Cait replied.

"Come on, *something's* going on, Cait. Are you okay?" David asked.

"I'm fine," she replied firmly. "Just...trust me on that. I'm okay. You don't need to be worried...I'm fine, all right?"

She looked back at the two of them, and he shared another glance with Ellie, who finally shrugged. "Okay, Cait, whatever you say."

He wanted to push it further, because *something* was up, but he also wanted to respect her privacy. What the fuck could it be, though? Apparently it involved Ashley, too. The thing was, Cait was a *really* open person. Or maybe she wasn't. Maybe he just got that impression of her because that's what she presented, and also because she talked about sex so freely, and that was something people normally kept to themselves.

What the fuck was it?! He felt like this was going to bug the shit out of him, but he made himself just relax. They had more important things to worry about and he had to remind himself that whatever it was, if it was his business, she'd *probably* share it with him. He trusted her that far. He trusted her a lot, given what had gone on between them so far, but this was just...out of character for her. Which just made him all the more curious.

"Shit," Ellie said.

"What?" Jennifer asked.

"I can see the second village...a lot of activity there. I think we should make them come to us, stay a good distance away and shoot them. I've got the best eyes among us. Cait, I know you're a good shot at a distance. David, Jennifer?"

"I'm not a great shot," Jennifer said. "I mean, I can do okay mid-to-close range..."

"I'm all right, but not great," David said. "At least, not with a pistol. If I had a rifle, on the other hand...but I'm just okay with a pistol."

"Fine. Save your ammo for when they get closer," Ellie replied.

They kept walking until they reached what Ellie judged to be the bare minimum distance required for her and Cait to make accurate shots. Cait pulled out her pistol and stood next to Ellie. Both of them took up a shooter's stance atop another small rise in the land. As they picked out targets, David studied the smaller village from afar.

It was maybe a third the size of the first one, little more than a tiny dock and maybe half a dozen shacks by the lake's edge. There were indeed several gray, skinny figures moving among the buildings, several of them crawling along the ground like oversized insects. They looked so horrifying, even from a distance.

He quickly studied the rest of the area, but there wasn't much to see. Trees and more trees, first along the left side of the road they had walked up, and then dead ahead, where the road disappeared into a forest. Though there were several larger buildings further up the coastline. He kept paying attention to the forest even as Ellie and Cait opened fire.

Anything could be drawn in by the noise and they were out in the open. He kept his pistol in hand and quickly double-checked it, making sure it was fully loaded and the safety was off. Once that was done, he glanced at the village.

All of the bulbous-headed figures were now

sprinting at an alarming speed towards them, making the distance between them disappear quickly, but there were definitely less of them now. More fell as they raced across the slush and dirt and snow. For the first fifteen seconds or so, David thought everything was going to be okay.

Ellie and Cait were excellent shots, hitting almost every single time they squeezed the trigger, and they were calm and measured in how they took down their targets, one by one.

And then something let out a wild roar from the forest, and David jerked back to face it, and saw a dozen shapes emerging from the woods.

"Wildcats!" he screamed.

Jennifer let out a shout of surprise.

"Deal with them!" Ellie snapped.

David took aim. They were so *fast*! He saw them, the awful things with their patchwork fur and decayed skin and long, vicious claws. They raced across the land between them even faster than the fucking vipers! He opened fire, trying to keep his hands steady.

The pistol jerked in his grasp as he started letting off shots, and Jennifer stepped up beside him, doing the same. The first round went wide, missing anything but the trees, but the second caught one of the wildcats in its misshapen forehead and dropped it.

He shifted aim, fired, fired, fired, dropped a second one, and saw a third go down with its head snapping backwards, a mist of corrupted blood escaping it as one of Jennifer's shots connected. Panic was fast approaching, though, because there was less distance and these things were *so fast*.

David emptied his pistol, trying not to fire wildly, and managed to put down another three of them. Hastily, he reloaded, and knew that they weren't going to be able to kill them all in time. "Incoming! Back up!" he screamed, and kept firing.

The wildcats and vipers hit them at roughly the same time.

The only good news was they'd managed to mostly wipe out the vipers, and between the two of them, he and Jennifer had taken down half the wildcats. The bad news was that that didn't matter nearly as much in close combat.

David buckled down and fought for his life.

He popped off another shot right in the face of the lead wildcat and turned its eye into a spray of chunky gore. He shifted and fired again, putting a shot into the open mouth of one of the mutated jags as it was roaring and coming for him. A third jumped at him and sent him sprawling, the gun flying from his hands.

He immediately went for his knife as he landed on his back, hearing Jennifer scream his name and a lot more gunfire. David managed to get the knife up and out right as the wildcat fell on him and he stabbed it through the eye. The thing went stiff and collapsed onto him, going slack, and he quickly shoved it off of himself.

Another one appeared over him, roaring its lungs out, and then its entire head disappeared as an almighty shotgun blast sounded. Looking up, he saw Cait standing over him as she twisted, shifting aim and firing again.

The muzzle flare nearly blinded him, the boom of the gun going off nearly deafening him, especially when she reloaded and did it a third time. His ears were ringing, but he sat up, blinking to get his eyesight back, trying to determine where the next attack would come from. Only the gunfire had fallen silent, and he saw no more attackers.

Merely a field of corpses.

"Are you okay?" Jennifer asked.

"Uh...I think so," he managed, feeling a little dazed.

Cait holstered her shotgun over her shoulder and crouched, her hands running slowly over him, checking him for wounds. "We good, Ellie?" she asked, frowning in concentration.

"We're good," Ellie replied. "Jennifer?"

"I'm fine," she replied, a little shakily.

"I think I'm fine, babe," David murmured.

"Just checking," Cait replied quietly. She checked his arms and legs, his torso, his head and neck, then smiled and nodded. She helped him up. "You're fine."

"Thanks," he replied.

"Here," Jennifer said. He looked over. She had his pistol in hand.

"Thanks," he replied, accepting it. He took a moment to wipe his knife off in the snow, then rubbed it down with a rag he carried around for just such an occasion and sheathed it, then he reloaded his pistol and looked around. They had done it, the vipers and the wildcats were dead, and he didn't see anything else lurking around.

"Well...that was close," Cait muttered.

"Yeah, but we fucked their shit up," Ellie replied. "Come on, let's go make sure the village is secure, then go back and deal with the rest of this."

"Wait," Cait said, and they stopped to look at her. "We're about as close as we're going to be to Lima Company. If we're going to talk to them, we should do it before we head back."

"We shouldn't keep them waiting," Ellie replied.

"Ellie, it's like a twenty minute walk from here, if that. They've already got their hands full with cleaning up their main village. We need to do this now, it just makes the most sense," Cait said.

She let out a short, frustrated growl. "Fine."

"Okay, thank you," Cait replied.

"Whatever." She turned and began stalking off towards the forest. David felt bad as they followed after her.

Today had been a very...trying day, for Ellie. And he was sure it wasn't going to get any better. But, apparently, that was the nature of their work.

He just hoped she didn't take a swing at one of them.

. . .

"So I don't actually know much about this Lima Company. Who are they exactly?" Jennifer asked as they walked through the woods.

They had managed to search over the half-dozen shacks without any real trouble, only having to put down a single viper that wasn't quite dead. There were no people, no survivors, and thankfully only one non-monster body.

Still miserable, but it could have been a lot worse. After securing the place as best they could, they left and began making their way south again, along the road that led into the woods, apparently where Lima Company rested their heads when they weren't out causing problems in the world at large.

"They're a group of ex-military personnel who still act like the military. I don't really know how many of them there are, sometimes I hear three dozen, sometimes fifty. I don't think anyone knows for sure," Cait explained. "From what I hear, they got here about two years ago, took over an abandoned military outpost, which is up ahead. For a while they helped people. Patrolled the area, killed monsters and bandits and raiders, offered protection for travelers sometimes, facilitated trades. But that's been stopping since I got here, about ten months ago. I guess it makes enough sense, given that's about the time the other types started showing up."

"They're run by an asshole named Stern," Ellie growled.

"You sound like you really hate him," Jennifer murmured.

"He *is* an asshole. Threatened to kill all three of us not all that long ago," David murmured.

"Holy shit, seriously?" Jennifer asked.

"Yeah, but he and his squad also saved our asses from a situation that probably would have killed us, and Ellie *did* point a gun at him..." Cait said.

"He was being a prick. He could have given us one of those solar panels," Ellie replied.

"Hey, I'm on your side," Cait replied. "But anyway, I have met his second in command, a woman named Lara. She's a lot more reasonable. I'm hoping to talk to her instead."

"Should I even be here? I mean, they won't like...shoot me, will they?" Jennifer asked nervously.

"No," Ellie replied. "Though we should keep our distance, for good measure. I don't really trust any of these shits."

None of them were sure what to say after that, so they just kept on walking through the forest. David glanced up, trying to gauge the position of the sun, and realized that it was a few hours past noon now.

Fuck, time was really flying.

Had they really been out here for like six or seven hours? It didn't seem right, surely it hadn't been that long, but...no. That was about right. Time was such a weird thing. David found his mind start to wander as they walked. He glanced at Jennifer. She had been pretty good in bed, and he was genuinely excited to have sex with her again.

Plus, it would be nice to introduce her to April and Evelyn.

There was something...vaguely uncomfortable about having sex with a woman without her meeting, or at least *knowing*, all three of his girlfriends. He supposed it felt somehow close to cheating, in a way, even if all parties consented to it happening, there was just something about it. Something that didn't sit right with him.

Speaking of vaguely uncomfortable sexual situations...

"Cait," he said.

"Yeah?" she replied.

"Am I crazy or is Amanda hitting on me?"

"Mrs. Carlson? No, you're not crazy. I saw her giving you the 'fuck me' eye more than once," Cait replied.

"*Mrs.* Carlson, huh?" Jennifer asked.

"Yep, she's a married woman living with her husband in the campgrounds," Cait said, looking extremely amused and self-satisfied.

He sighed. "I didn't know you were gonna give me shit about this."

"I'm not giving you shit, just...it's amusing. I mean, right?"

"Yeah, it's amusing," Ellie agreed.

"Do you think it means anything?"

"Why? You want to fuck her, don't you?" Cait asked.

"Duh."

"You don't think she's a little old for you?" Ellie asked.

"No," he replied. "I'd fucking love to go to bed with a noticeably older woman."

"Yeah, I can see the appeal. And she is fucking hot. Still pretty fit. And she's got a *great* ass. God, do I love watching that woman's ass," Cait murmured.

"So would you fuck her? If she came onto you?" Jennifer asked.

"*If* her husband was cool with it, then yeah, definitely. Something about her...I think that woman can *fuck,* you know?"

"Oh yeah. As a woman who can just fuck for days, I can recognize that in another woman," Cait replied confidently. "If I had to guess, and I say this was no malice and only love, I'd say Amanda was a straight up *slut* in her younger days, probably for a while, and she still likes to slut around with cute younger guys whenever she finds an opportunity. And again, I say that with no malice. I know a lot of people have trouble with the word slut," Cait said. "But I get the feeling Amanda would appreciate it...I mean, you know, were we in the proper setting and more comfortable around each other."

"That makes sense, I guess," David murmured after considering it.

"Maybe I could talk with her. Have some wine one of these nights..." Cait said.

"Do we *have* wine?" Ellie asked.

"Yeah. I've got a bottle stashed there. Like thirty years old. I've been meaning to have a drink, one of these nights," she replied. She frowned suddenly.

"Then again, maybe not..."

"You've been holding out on me, huh?" Ellie asked.

"What? No. I told you."

"When?!"

"Like two weeks ago, during the first blizzard...I think. Or maybe not. Fuck, I don't know. I've been so busy recently..."

"Well, whatever, if you do pop the cork, let me know."

"Yeah. I will." David glanced at her. She looked distracted again.

Suddenly, the trees fell away from them, opening up into two huge fields of mud and snow and dead bushes. To the right, the lake. To the left, eventually, more trees, and the bulk of the mountain. Dead ahead, the military base. The road terminated at its front gates. It certainly looked like a base, almost like a fortress. A wall of metal plates surrounded it, no doubt welded together with professional precision, and there were two watchtowers built at the entrance gate, behind the wall, connected by a bridge over the gate.

He could see a person up there, a single figure against the backdrop of the three-story building that the metal wall protected. They were motionless, from what he could tell, staring directly at them, though not pointing anything their way.

"So was this always a military outpost?" David asked as they slowly walked up the road.

"I'm honestly not sure, but I don't think so. I think it was some kind of storage building, or maybe a factory or something. What I think happened was, at some point over the past twenty years, a group came here and turned it into one, found big, solid metal plates and welded them together into a defensible wall, built the watchtowers, and then, for some reason, at some point, abandoned it. Or maybe they were all killed? Dunno. But I think Lima Company rolled through, found it, decided to set up shop and make a home for themselves," Ellie explained. "But that could be bullshit. Honestly, history isn't anyone's strong suit around here. Myth is closer, sometimes."

"Hmm."

As they drew closer, he noticed Jennifer stuck behind him, and he let her, encouraging it, even. Again, that wildcard element. He didn't intend to let anyone hurt her, but...he looked around, this was admittedly a pretty bad place to get caught. Way too much open space, nowhere to run, nowhere to hide. No wonder they'd set up shop here.

"Hello, Ellie," the woman atop the watchtower said.

"Lara. Thank God," Ellie replied, sounding relieved. "We were hoping to talk with you."

"Were you now? It's been quite a while since I've seen you. Hi, Cait. I see you've brought some friends with you," the woman, Lara, replied. David was relieved to hear that she sounded actually amicable, and not that weird, veiled, vague-threatening 'amicable' that people like Colonel Stern or Murray put on.

"Yes. These are my friends. David, and Jennifer. This is Lieutenant Lara Hale," Ellie said, making introductions.

"Pleased to meet you," David said, while Jennifer offered a quiet 'Hi'. He found himself staring up at a pale woman with sharp green eyes and short brown hair who carried a rifle and looked *exceptionally* good in the camouflage uniform she was wearing.

"And you. What's up?" she asked.

"We need your help," Ellie replied.

"Oh. Well...shit. I might not really be in a position to help," she replied awkwardly, frowning.

"I know. Just...hear me out. The thieves, the ones that have been harassing people, the ones who burned down River View, we're going to kill them," Ellie said.

She was silent for a few moments, then began to open her mouth to respond. Instead, she looked behind her, like she'd heard something, then quickly looked back and muttered, "Fuck...maybe you guys should go."

"Why?" Ellie asked, tensing.

"What's going on up there, Lieutenant?" an unfortunately familiar voice asked from somewhere behind the gate.

"Visitors. *Friendly* visitors," Lara replied, stressing that fact.

"Friendly visitors, huh? Well, I would like to know what they want."

Lara sighed softly. A moment later, Colonel Stern appeared beside her after climbing up to the watchtower. "Ah. Ellie. Cait. And friends."

"Stern," Ellie growled.

"What brings you out here to my home on this glorious winter day?" he asked. For a moment, nobody spoke. Ellie seemed extremely reluctant to continue. "You must have come all this way out here for a reason," he pressed, smiling down at them.

"We're looking for help," David said finally, stepping forward, because he was the one who'd insisted on this, so he should have to put up with the conversation. "We're going after the group burned down River View and has continued to harass basically everyone in the region. Obviously, we would benefit greatly from even a few soldiers from your unit."

"Yes, you would," Stern murmured, considering it.

"Colonel, if we could eliminate these jackasses, it *would* be a large improvement to the whole region," Lara said. "I do believe that was our goal, right?"

"Of course. And that hasn't changed. However...I must regretfully decline. We have more important tasks to deal with at present. I do wish you luck, though."

He turned and began walking back to the ladder. David felt anger welling up within him and before he could think better of it, snapped, "You're a fucking coward, Stern!"

The Colonel froze, and Lara looked down at him with wide, anxious eyes. He turned around, and David thought he would see anger on his face, but he didn't. If anything, he saw surprise. It reminded him of the expression the man had worn when Ellie had threatened him back at the bunker, over the solar panels.

"How's that, son?" he replied, taking a few steps closer. He almost looked amused.

"You and yours stay locked up here, safe and secure behind your fucking wall, and if something isn't bothering you, well then, it's not a fucking problem, is it? You'd watch the world burn and warm your hands by the fire so long as it isn't burning you. You keep talking about how you're here to help people, but every chance you get, you turn your fucking nose up at us. So I say you're a coward, Stern," David replied, a shocking amount of anger boiling around in him.

Stern looked amused, then actually regretful, though not guilty. "You're what...twenty four? Twenty five?"

"Twenty five," David replied curtly.

"You're young, and you've got guts. Like Ellie. Like Cait. I'll give you that. And I appreciate that. I remember what it was like to be your age, full of piss and vinegar. But you don't see the bigger picture, and I'm not particularly inclined to show you. Suffice to say, there are bigger problems to deal with."

"Let me go with them," Lara said. "I doubt I'd be gone for more than a day."

Stern opened his mouth, then paused as a very strange sound, what sounded like talking, but heavily distorted talking, emerged from somewhere near him. At first, David had no idea what the fuck was happening, but then watched as he reached into his pocket and pulled out a small black device, then brought it to his mouth.

"Say again?"

The same sound was repeated, and it was slightly clearer this time, but David couldn't make out the words. It was a radio, he realized. He knew what they were, he'd seen them before and knew (roughly) how they worked, but it had been a while since he'd actually seen one. Although he thought he remembered the doctors mentioning they had one.

"Understood. I'm on my way." He pocketed the radio. "No, Lieutenant. The matter's closed. And where is the other guard?" he snapped.

"Piss break," Lara replied.

He sighed. "I'll deal with him later. Goodbye," he said, tossing another glance at the group, then he turned and left, heading back down the ladder.

Lara watched him go and after about a minute,

waved them closer. They walked closer until they were at the gate itself, looking straight up at Lara, who looked down at them. "Listen," she said, keeping her voice down, "I will help you. When do you need me?"

"Do you know where the old campgrounds are, southwest of River View?" David asked. She nodded. "Come there, tomorrow, just before sundown. Come prepared."

"I will. Goodbye, and good luck."

"Thank you," Ellie said. Lara nodded curtly, then motioned for them to leave.

The four of them began making their way away from the military outpost. When they had reached the trees again, Cait said, "Well, that went better than expected."

Ellie just grunted, and they continued their journey back to the fishing village.

CHAPTER EIGHT

The next hour passed without too much trouble.

They walked back through the forest and took a moment to stop by the secondary village once more, just to double check. Only a few zombies had showed up, and they were put down with ease.

They checked the water as much as they could, but either there were vipers and they were hiding well, or there weren't. Either way, the crew had done what they had intended to do, and moved on. They made the walk back to the primary village without running into anything else, and it turned out to be a relatively pleasant walk.

By the time they made it back to the main village, a surprising amount of progress had been made. Not only were most of the bodies shifted, the viper corpses all being tossed into a pile about fifty feet away from the settlement, but the amount of people had doubled.

They were in the process of picking up the pieces, already beginning repairs to their village. They were hard workers, it seemed. He imagined having access to presumably a few great fishing spots would give them quite the command of commerce, like the farmers.

Murray was standing in the middle of it all, directing the people like a foreman. He looked very in his element, and he smiled as he saw them approaching.

"So, I take it you have succeeded?" he asked.

"Yeah," David replied. "We killed everything that was there. We didn't see any people, though there was one dead body, I don't know if it was one of yours or not. But when we left, it had been cleared of anything undead."

"Excellent!" He turned. "Elias! Get over here!" Then he turned back to them as a man with a plain face and a thin build came over. His chin-length brown hair was a mess and he was filthy from no doubt lots of work and running around through the forest over the past few days, but he seemed in decent spirits at least.

"Yes, Murray?" he asked.

"These people are here to take you to the doctors to continue our agreement." He looked at them closely. "You get him safely there and back here again, and you'll get Ruby. Not before."

"Yes, yes, Murray," Ellie replied. "We'll get the job done. You got any firepower, Elias?"

"No," he replied.

She sighed.

"He's not the best shot," Murray said.

"Fine. Just stay close to us, stay quiet, and keep up. Got it?"

"Yes," he replied.

"Good. Let's go."

Ellie set off back out of the village, and they followed her, and once more they were off, again heading back the way they'd initially come.

It, too, was a mercifully uneventful trip. Though it wasn't all a mercy. It left David with a lot of time to think. He kept wondering about Cait, if she was okay, if something was wrong, if it was something *he'd* done to upset her or worry her or...something. The problem was, he genuinely had no idea.

There was so little to go off of, but he kept coming back to the concern that maybe something was wrong with her. She'd suddenly needed to go to the doctors for a 'checkup', and acted dodgy about it, and had been extremely distracted ever since her visit. What had they told her? He had yet to have a lover outright die on him…

And it was something he hoped never to endure, though he knew that was basically impossible, unless he died before all his other lovers, which was becoming an increasingly populated pool. He worried over it the whole way back to the hospital, and didn't feel any closer to understanding it.

He was still considering it when they got to the hospital and were let in through the front door. Donald was waiting for them.

"Ah, Elias! I'm so glad you're here," he said. "Are you okay?"

"I'm fine, doc," Elias replied.

"The village was indeed attacked by a huge pack of vipers," Ellie said.

"Oh dear," Donald murmured.

"Yeah. Most of them made it out okay, and we helped them clear it out, so all should be well," Ellie replied. "Go do your thing, we gotta escort him back, too."

"Oh. Yes. Are you ready, Elias?" Donald asked.

"Uh...yeah, I'm ready," he replied.

"Good, please come along."

David watched them head into the infirmary, briefly toying around with the idea of asking Donald or one of the other staff about whatever they'd told Cait, but he immediately rejected it. Not only would they likely not tell him, it would be wrong. He wanted to give her her privacy, he was just so fucking *worried*.

As he and the other three began waiting around in the main room, he heard heavy footsteps coming from the only other doorway in the room, and the goliath woman, Vanessa, appeared in the door, having to duck a little to step in. She stared intently at him for a few seconds, and he felt caught in her gaze. She was *very* intimidating, and not just because she was probably approaching almost two feet taller than he was.

Finally, she looked at the others. "Ladies, I'd like a word with you."

"What about?" Ellie asked.

"You'll see," Vanessa replied, and turned around, disappearing back into the room she'd come from. Jennifer followed after her, as did Ellie. Cait lingered for a moment, looking at David, who looked back at her with a questioning glance.

"Don't worry, babe, just wait here for a moment, okay?"

"...all right," he replied.

David sighed, now finding himself alone in the main room. He walked around slowly, checking out the furniture, not really sure where this was going. Hopefully there wasn't some new security concern, but she'd looked at him in a pretty specific way. He walked over to the front door and peered out through the little slot there, staring at the snowy landscape beyond, and wondered exactly how many undead things were hanging out in even the nearest square mile radius to his current position. The number would probably turn his stomach.

There always seemed to be more of them.

After another moment, Ellie returned and she had that smirk on her face. "Come on," she said, beckoning him closer.

"What's up?" he asked, crossing the room.

"You've got another admirer."

"Wait, fucking seriously?" he asked.

"Yeah. Vanessa likes you. She wants a quickie upstairs. Given we're all intimate with you, and one of us is actually dating you, and one of us is kinda-sorta dating *her,* she thought it only polite to make sure this was all good."

"*I'm* the one she's wanting to fuck, didn't she think to ask me first? What if I said no?" he asked as they headed into the other room. At its back was a stairwell, and this is where she led him.

"Shockingly, David, ladies like myself and Cait and Vanessa have gotten quite good at reading people, especially people who want to fuck us. It's...*very* obvious. Especially on young men. You've wanted to fuck Vanessa from the moment she entered your field of vision. Or am I wrong?"

He sighed as they headed upstairs. "No, you aren't wrong."

"And there you have it. That's why. So fuck her, have some fun, let us watch, and hopefully by the time you're done, Elias will be done with his donation and we can go." She stopped, then snickered suddenly.

"What?" he asked.

"He's donating blood, you're donating sperm," she replied.

He chuckled. "I guess so."

They passed through a room that looked like a kitchen and dining room, through a door at the back that led directly into what he guessed was Vanessa's bedroom. Or her bedroom that she apparently shared with someone else, as there were two beds in the room, one much larger. She was sitting on the end of it, completely naked, and Cait, Jennifer, and Katya were gathered around her. Cait and Katya sat on the other bed, Jennifer in a chair nearby.

"Wow," he said.

"Yep," Ellie replied, closing the door behind them.

"I take it she filled you in," Vanessa said.

"Yes. You intend to have me...fill you in," he replied.

Cait and Katya began laughing.

"You're right, I like him," Katya said.

"You're all really gonna watch?" he asked as he took his backpack off.

"Duh," Katya replied. "I watch Vanessa and Jennifer fuck all the time now."

"All right then." He set his backpack on the floor, got out of his shirt and his boots and his pants and boxers, leaving them all in a pile.

"You left your socks on," Jennifer murmured.

"He does that a lot," Cait replied.

"They aren't impeding me, and it's fucking cold, even in here, on the floor," David replied as he stepped up to Vanessa.

God, she was so *tall*.

Even sitting down, she was the same height as him standing up. It was incredibly intoxicating, intimidating, and erotic, all at once. She had some big breasts. Honestly, they were probably the biggest he'd ever seen. Her body type struck him as what would happen if Evelyn dedicated herself to working out all the time.

She had some cut muscles, but also had some heft to her. Especially in the lower half, with thighs and hips to fucking die for. Her pussy, in between those huge, firm thighs of hers, was freshly shaved, with just a dusting of pale blonde stubble.

For a few moments, they just looked at each

other.

Vanessa had an oddly beautiful face. It was very...angular, very rough. She had high cheekbones and a scar across her cheek, and another on her forehead. Her hair was so pale blonde, pulled into a rough ponytail now, and her eyes were extremely bright and blue.

"Intimidated?" she asked.

"Very," he replied.

She glanced down. "Obviously not *that* intimidated," she murmured, reaching out and wrapping her long fingers around his cock. He shivered and exhaled sharply at her touch.

"I think, to David, intimidation is an aphrodisiac," Ellie said.

"God, don't ever let him negotiate anything for your group then," Vanessa murmured.

David snorted. "It would only be a problem if I was negotiating with an attractive woman," he replied.

"I'll have to keep that in mind," Ellie said.

"I hear you have a goliath girlfriend," Vanessa murmured, massaging his cock now. She had a *big* fucking hand.

"Yeah," he managed. "Evie."

"I imagine you fuck her often, huh?"

"Yes. Pretty much every night. We share a bed more often than not," he replied.

"You got a thing for tall women?"

"Very much so."

She laughed. "You must have *quite* the thing for me then. I'm almost eight feet tall."

"Yes. That's true."

"Then let's get this show started."

She pulled him a little closer to her and kissed

him on the mouth. He kissed her back, taking her huge breasts in his hands and groping them, immediately in lust with how they felt, with the act of trying and utterly failing to get his hands wrapped around them.

They were bigger than his head. She slipped her tongue smoothly into his mouth as they kissed and she continued to massage his stiff cock, working it slowly in her grasp. He eagerly responded with his own tongue, twisting with hers. She had an interesting taste, kind of dark, kind of smoky, something that made his heart race a little faster. She almost tasted of danger and excitement.

"Okay," she said, breaking the kiss after a moment. "Unfortunately, I don't have a lot of time to play, so..." She laid back on the bed and opened her legs a bit more. "Fuck away. When I come, you can come."

"All right," he replied, stepping closer to her and lining up his cock. "Do I have to pull out?"

"No. Pump me full," she replied.

"Oh fuck yes," he whispered, and slid into her. She let out a moan as he did, as did he, though the groan that escaped him was louder.

She was *wet*. So fucking wet.

"He *loves* busting inside of ladies," Ellie murmured.

"Who fucking wouldn't?" David groaned as he settled his hands on her absolutely enormous, broad, firm hips and began sliding in and out of her, began fucking her. She had an incredible slickness to her, a wonderful heat that began to fill him with pleasure. His cock throbbed in response to the attention and he was soon pushed to thrusting into her more rapidly, sliding smoothly and quickly in and out of that amazing goliath vagina.

He was fucking a nearly eight foot tall woman.

It was utterly unreal, even after the sex he'd had with Evelyn. When it came to height and size, it was like even an extra few inches was an exponential factor of growth. He found his eyes crawling restlessly across her huge body. Her well-muscles arms, her enormous breasts that swayed and jiggled with each impact of his hips into hers.

Her beautiful face, with its curious attributes of rough, rugged beauty, and her ghostly eyes. And her hips. His hands on her hips, which were easily twice as wide as his own, maybe even three times as wide as his own.

Making love to her was like a dream. She felt less like a fellow inhuman that inhabited the Earth just like him, and more like some kind of mythical creature that had stepped straight out of a legend.

A sex deity or a warrior angel, huge and powerful and almighty.

And she was enjoying this.

"You've clearly had a lot of practice," she moaned. "You've got a great rhythm, and your body reacts to mine nicely...you were right, Cait, he has a pleasant thickness."

"He looks like he's high or something," Katya murmured.

"That's my pussy. He's in love with it, aren't you, David?" Vanessa asked.

"Fuck...yes..." he moaned and started going harder and faster, sliding frantically in and out of her. He knew he needed to make her come, and that he should be going slower, because if he kept on this path it would send him careening into his own orgasm, but he just could *not* stop fucking hammering away at this amazing pussy.

It seriously felt beyond fantastic.

Coming back to himself a bit, David laid his thumb on her clit and began to rub it. She immediately jerked and shuddered and let out a cry of pleasure.

"You found her fuck button, all right," Katya said.

"Don't you *dare* stop!" Vanessa demanded, clenching her fists and releasing them repeatedly as he simultaneously screwed her and stimulated her clit.

He didn't dare stop, and was rewarded with an orgasm from her hardly half a minute later.

Vanessa orgasmed like a goddess.

Her whole body got in on it and she had more control than most women he had been with. That made enough sense, given her size relative to pretty much everyone else. At just about eight feet tall *and* strong as fuck, it must be really easy to accidentally hurt people.

She closed her eyes and let out a loud, low moan of pure bliss, clenching her thighs as a powerful but controlled shudder of total sexual gratification ran through her body, making her huge breasts bounce.

He felt her vaginal muscles constrict around his cock as he continued fucking her, felt her shifting her hips in his grasp, felt that hot release of feminine sex juices as she came, and the wet heat was nearly overwhelming in its added pleasure.

He fucked her harder, and faster, and quickly gave up the losing battle of holding off his own orgasm. David let out a cry of almost surprised bliss as his own climax began with a bang, the first of his seed leaving him in a hard contraction of pure pleasure.

He dug his fingertips in, moaning her name several times as his seed left him in furious spurts. Each time his cock kicked inside of her, a fresh wave of blindingly powerful rapture roared through him, emanating from his core and reaching out to every part of his body.

He did precisely as she had demanded and pumped that amazingly perfect goliath vagina full of his seed as hot pink ecstasy ensnared and unified them.

It was glorious.

And then the orgasms were wearing out, and soon they were left panting, him more than her, and his legs trembled, and he slowly pulled out of her and sat down beside her on the bed.

"Wow," Katya murmured. "You were right."

"Told you," Cait replied.

"Right about what?" he murmured.

"You look really good when you fuck," Katya replied.

"Oh. Uh, thanks," he said, which made most of the women in the room laugh.

"You're right about that, too. Cait said you were still kind of awkward about sex," Katya said.

"Well, she's not wrong. Before this month, I didn't have a whole hell of a lot of experience," David replied. He groaned as he stood up and popped his neck and back and shoulders. "Fuck, I'm tired. Meeting Ellie and Cait and Evelyn and April and Jennifer really changed that for me. They're all so...eager. That alone makes whatever I endured to get to this point worth it."

"Oh really?" Katya asked, laughing softly. "They're that good at sex?"

"Given what you look like, you probably never

had to endure years and years of sexual isolation. Given what you *all* look like. Except you Jennifer. And obviously I'm not saying you're unattractive, you know I don't think that, I'm just acknowledging the fact that you're a wraith. Sex isn't everything, I'm not stupid enough to think that, but it is a lot. Well, sex with the right people, anyway. And so far, the people I've met here are the right people. So yes, worth it."

"I've *definitely* had my dry spells, and more than one guy turn me down flat," Katya replied after a moment.

"Yeah, but I'm guessing those dry spells had more to do with where you were or your own mood rather than trying and failing. Everyone gets rejected, well, except probably Cait, but I think any of you could find someone to share a bed with every night without all that much effort." He paused. "Okay, except for Vanessa. I think you're *insanely* attractive, but I can appreciate the fact that, at almost eight feet in height, you probably scare the shit out of most people."

"Yeah," she replied.

"I guess you're not wrong, at least on my account," Cait murmured.

Ellie sighed. "Yeah, when I'm alone it's because I want to be. I can't honestly say that offers of sex haven't ever outweighed my desires for sex."

He looked over at Katya, who stared back at him. She seemed to be considering his words. "It's hard to say," she replied finally. "I've never felt particularly attractive, but most of the time I've not cared. Sometimes not caring is easy, and it's gotten easier with age. Although this doesn't help matters," she said, tracing the scar down the side of her face, staring below her right eye and extending to a little past her jaw.

"I don't know about that," David replied.

She laughed. "Well yeah, some people like scars. Especially face scars, for some reason. But usually on men. It's less appealing on women, I've been told. But I've had more than my fair share of offers, if I'm being honest. Of course that's its own problem. Maybe that's our biggest disconnect. You guys look at us girls getting hit on all the time and feel envy. How great would it be to get requests for straight-up sex almost every day? We look at you guys and think, 'fuck, wouldn't it be great to just get left the fuck alone most days?' Guys and girls who aren't...conventionally attractive."

"You mean us ugly girls," Vanessa said.

"You are *not* ugly," Katya replied immediately.

"You're definitely not," Jennifer murmured.

"Fuck no you're not," David said.

She snorted and rolled her eyes. "Fine, not 'conventionally attractive'. Of course I suppose my problem is that I *am* considered *quite* attractive among my own kind. I'm just not interested in my own kind. I've got *such* a taste for you smaller people. No idea why. But it sure narrows the field quite a bit...anyway, thanks for the sex, David. It was pretty good. I've got work to do."

"Oh. Yeah. Uh, you're welcome, and thank you very much for the sex. It was fucking amazing," he replied.

She smirked and stood. "Well now I feel bad with my 'pretty good' comment. But I'm glad that you found it as good as you did. We'll have to do it again sometime."

"Yes. Definitely," he agreed.

She walked over to a washbasin and began cleaning up. David sat back down and yawned. "Fuck, I'm *really* tired," he muttered.

"Well, you've probably got about another half hour at least," Katya said. "He'll need some time to recover after getting the blood drawn. Even that might be pushing it."

Ellie sighed. She'd since gotten to her feet and had begun to pace restlessly. "David," she said, "we should do the scouting now."

"Should we?" he asked uncertainly.

"Yes. We have time, we're as close as we're going to be. We should take the opportunity and get it done now," Ellie replied.

He considered it for a moment, then nodded. "Yeah, all right. You're right." David stood and began pulling his clothes back on.

"Do you have binoculars I could borrow?" Ellie asked.

"Yeah," Vanessa said. "Katya, in my pack."

"Yep," Katya replied, and got up. David finished getting dressed and pulled his pack back on. Ellie accepted a pair of small binoculars from Katya, securing them in her pocket. As soon as she was done, she turned to face David.

"You ready?" she asked.

"Ready," he replied.

"Then let's go."

"Good luck," Cait said, and Jennifer stepped closer and they each gave him and Ellie a hug and a kiss. Then they were off.

...

"So that was...interesting," David said.

They'd been walking for about ten minutes and had finally reached the path that ran in between the river and the forest. They'd debated briefly about how to tackle heading to where they wanted to scout, and Ellie had won out. There was the possibility of getting attacked by vipers, but the risk of running into stalkers, who seemed to absolutely own this part of the region, was much greater, so they'd decided to risk the river.

"That's one way of looking at it," Ellie replied. "I knew Vanessa was going to make a jump at you if she met you. Expect a similar treatment from Katya."

"You think?" he asked.

"Yeah. Stop being surprised by this."

"Why!? It's surprising. I believe I made my point back in the bedroom."

"I suppose so. I suppose, from your perspective, it would be, but from mine, it isn't. You just apparently haven't been around the right people for your adult life. The right women. Or maybe you just weren't the right sort of person. This is how it is with...for want of a better term, people of action. You're becoming a man of action, and are throwing in your lot with women of action. People who *act,* who make decisions and enact them. Being decisive and having convictions and making choices, while being tempered with modesty, is...*shockingly* attractive, David."

"Is it really?" he asked, considering it. He saw it as quite attractive in the women he knew. Capability, confidence, competence, it was very hot in Cait and Ellie and Evelyn. They were so...certain, so determined, without seemingly like they held it over you or thought they were better than you. Most of the time.

"Of course it is. Everyone's so fucking scared now, and it's not even like I blame them. We live in a world where some jackass in a bad mood can pull out a gun and shoot you in the face and probably get away with it, and with literal monsters that roam the landscape and want nothing more than to rip your guts out. So an overabundance of caution isn't unwarranted. And yet...that honestly makes bravery and decisive action even more attractive. I'm going to be just totally honest: watching you stand up to Stern and call him a coward, call him out on his bullshit, it got me wet. Like seriously, it made me horny."

"For real? You don't think I was being...petulant? Or stupid? Arrogant?"

"Fuck no. And not just because I hate his guts. That was brave. Stupid, maybe. Risky is more like it. But I think Lara agreed to do what she agreed to do only because you stood up to him. I think she was on the fence, and that decided her. Helping us out is very risky. She knows me and Cait, but doing something like this...Stern could exile or even execute her for this. She had to feel like it was a risk worth taking. Lara's a good person. She cares about people. If I thought she'd do it, I'd ask her to sign up with our group."

"It's too bad she won't," he murmured.

Ellie laughed. "You just say that because you want to fuck her."

"That's not the *only* reason I say that," David replied.

"It's all right. I want to fuck her, too. So does Cait. I'm still not sure if she does girls. Maybe we'll find out someday. Speaking of which, Jennifer is *really* into you. I mean, I figured she'd like you after you slept together, but I've *never* seen her like this before. She's so...jubilant. So excited. I think you might have another inhuman lady on your hands. I wouldn't be surprised if we could talk her into moving in with us."

"Really? She seemed to like her house..."

"She does, but I think you reminded her of what it's like to be around people that are *nice* to her. She's obviously come back out of her shell a lot around the doctors, and I'm pretty sure she connects that to you. She would never have even gone to them if we didn't come ask for her help, and you left the biggest impression on her of all of us, so...yeah, I think she associates her recent social resurgence with you strongly, and that makes her like you even more powerfully than she would have otherwise. How do you feel about her?"

"I like her," he replied. "I'd like to spend more time with her, get to know her better, but I like her. She's...sweet. She reminds me a little of April."

"Yeah, I can see that. Less timid, but yeah," Ellie said. She paused. "Okay, hush. We're going to have to head back into the woods now."

David nodded and clammed up. She led him to a path that led back into the woodlands. They'd managed to make it a decent distance up the river, ideally bypassing a lot of stalker territory, but it was genuinely hard to tell what belonged to the stalkers and what didn't at this point. And now they had the vipers to worry about, apparently. He wanted to believe that it was a fluke, and that was possible, but it seemed unlikely.

Maybe those were the threats that Stern was referring to.

Or perhaps there was something else that he wasn't seeing. David thought about it for the first few minutes as they made their way through the stands of dead trees, but ultimately shook the thoughts off. Now was the time to pay attention.

If they were very lucky, they could scout out the jerks, make some notes, get back to the hospital, escort Elias back home, and then get back home all before the sun had gone down. It seemed unlikely, but not impossible.

He followed Ellie through the woods, trusting her. She seemed to know exactly where they were going and what she was doing, and he was careful to make as little noise as possible. Minutes went by in the frigid air as they pressed on.

David studied his surroundings. He saw dead trees and snow, mostly, but occasionally he caught sight of a distant zombie, or, a few times, some animals. A deer here, a rabbit there, several big black birds staring down on them from above, and that made him think of the other kind of undead that he had yet to encounter, thankfully. The hunters. They were the only ones that flew, as they were mutated AVs.

He hoped never to see one.

They walked until they reached a hilly part of the land, where the landscape went off in unexpected dips and rises, and Ellie warned him softly to watch his step. He kept close to her as the trees seemed to press in.

He wondered where they were going first, what he would see. He had never been to this part of the region. He knew there were still places unexplored to him, still things to discover and experience. Exploration had always been something he had a particular love of. Buildings, places, old vehicles, unique and beautiful locations in the landscape.

Finding them was always a joy, and even searching a new building was its own joy.

Abruptly, the trees fell away, and suddenly he was given a fantastic view, perhaps the best he'd had since coming to this region, of a vast valley that spread out below him. It was a few hundred feet deep and a few miles long, stretching off to the north, away from where they stood at its head, atop a cliff sheer that served as its southern end.

"Holy shit," he whispered.

"Beautiful, isn't it?" Ellie murmured.

"Uh-huh."

"It's roughly a thousand times more beautiful in the spring and summer."

She crouched and retrieved the binoculars, then began studying the valley floor. David did the same, without the added benefit. Mostly he saw trees and flat land, but two things stuck out. They were both about a quarter ways down the valley ahead of them. The first was a half-constructed building. It was surrounded by the rusted-out hulks of huge vehicles and machinery. He saw an old bulldozer, a few pickup trucks, and a crane that might have been covered in dead vines.

The other curiosity was a hole that at first looked like a cave in the valley wall directly west of the half-constructed building, but he then realized it was manmade. It was framed by rusted girders, bracing the rock and earth. All of it looked long abandoned.

"Well, I don't think they're here," Ellie said finally. "I see zero activity around the building or the mine."

"What is this place?" David asked.

"A mining operation, an old one, back from when the world wasn't overrun by undead. Not sure what the building was going to be, maybe an HQ for the mining op, but obviously they never got a chance to finish it."

"Anyone ever check it out? The mine?" he asked. She replaced the binoculars. "Yes."

"And?"

"They don't come back."

"Oh."

"Yep. Something bad's down there. Come on. This place is dead. I figured it would be a long shot anyway that even they would be stupid enough to establish camp down in that valley. The next place is the most likely."

"What is it?" he asked as they resumed walking.

"Hunting grounds."

He fell silent as they trudged on through the snow and dead plants. They skirted the top edge of the valley until they had passed it, then plunged back into the dead forest. The minutes again ticked by with an annoying slowness. They walked and walked, then walked some more, pausing occasionally as Ellie heard something or thought she saw something, but ultimately, they remained undisturbed all the way to the hunting grounds.

"Okay," Ellie whispered, "stop." He froze, and she stood frozen beside him, waiting, listening. Suddenly, a grin split her face, a dark one. "Hear that?"

"Yes," he replied softly. Voices. Several voices.

"Come on. Slowly, quietly."

They crept forward until they reached an incline in the land, and soon they got down onto their bellies and crawled through the snow. Finally, they crested it, and that's when David saw them. Ahead of them, perhaps three hundred feet away, was an encampment. Essentially it was a collection of cabins built around a structure maybe half the size of the main office he now called home back at the campgrounds.

The place was definitely well-populated. He saw a few dozen people moving around. Some guarded the perimeter, some sat at fires in the middle of the area, some were dragging in fresh game kills, some were gutting and skinning them. He could see more through what windows he could view from his position.

"Is it them?" he whispered.

"It's them," Ellie murmured.

"You're *sure?*"

"Yes. Look at the guy near the biggest fire."

She passed him the binoculars and he studied the man in question. There were several sitting there, drinking from mugs, cheering and jeering in equal measure as they talked, and he recognized the man who had led the assault on his home two weeks ago.

"Yeah, I see the fucker," he growled, passing them back.

"Good. Let's study up for another few minutes, then get the fuck back to the hospital. We're gonna nail these fuckers," Ellie replied.

CHAPTER NINE

They made it back to the hospital without a problem and in good time.

By then, Elias was just about ready to go.

"So?" Vanessa asked as they came into the side room with the stairs. "You find them?"

"Fuck yes, we did. They're at the hunting grounds. Dozens of them. It's definitely them. I think we can make this work if we go hard and fast," Ellie replied.

"Good. Count me in. When are we doing this?" Vanessa replied.

"Tomorrow night. Be ready for a full goddamned assault."

"Oh, I'll be ready. You can fucking believe that. Think I'll take the time to pull the Widowmaker out of storage and clean her up."

"Widowmaker?" David asked.

Vanessa just grinned savagely. "You'll see."

Cait appeared in the doorway. "Elias is ready."

"All right. Remember, tomorrow night. We'll probably be here around sundown."

"I'll be ready," Vanessa replied.

They gathered Jennifer and Elias, and then they left. Once again, they trekked as quickly as they could through the snow and the trees. Conversation was minimal and their pace was as fast as Ellie could make it. Elias seemed a little out of it, and David wondered how much blood they'd taken. No wonder he needed an escort.

This time, they did run into a pair of stalkers and a few zombies. They dispatched them handily though, and by the time they got back to the fishing village, the place was bustling with activity, and the number of people had again doubled. He thought that everyone in the village had returned by now.

They tracked down Murray, who was overseeing some repairs.

"Ah, I see you've held up your end of the bargain," he said upon seeing them and Elias.

"Can I go lay down now?" Elias murmured.

"Yeah, go on."

"Thanks," he said quietly, and drifted away.

"Well, Murray? We held up our end of the bargain," Ellie said.

"Yes, yes. Don't worry, so will I. Ruby!" he called. A moment later a jag woman with vividly red fur approached from among the shacks. She really stood out among the group, not only because of her fur, but also because of how tall and lean she was. She was probably six four or six five, and very skinny, though he could see that her frame was packed with small but well-defined muscles. She had brilliantly green eyes.

"Yes?" she asked.

"They did the job, so you're with them for their operation. Don't get yourself killed out there," Murray said.

"Yeah, sure," she replied, and turned to face them. "Ellie. Cait. Good to see you." She spoke with a clipped professionalism that he thought might be coldness, but then realized was more just how she was.

"Ruby," Ellie replied. "This is David, and this is Jennifer."

"Good to meet you," she said, nodding tightly to them. They both responded in kind. "So, what's this about? Murray was not very forthcoming with details."

"You know the group that attacked River View and burned it to the ground?" Cait asked. Ruby nodded again. "We're going to murder them."

"Ah. Then I stand ready to assist you in full. I trust you'll be wanting to put me to use as a sniper," she replied.

"Yes, we were hoping to do that," Ellie replied. "They're at the hunting lodge. Would you like to come with us, back to the campgrounds?"

Ruby hesitated. She looked around at the other villagers. "I would like to, but I can't. Not right now. There's too much to do here. When is this happening?" she asked.

"Tomorrow night."

"Okay. Where would it be best that I met you?"

"The hospital," Ellie replied. "Be there at sundown."

"Understood. I'll be there. It was good seeing you all, I have to get back to work now."

"Okay, goodbye, Ruby."

"Goodbye."

She turned and left.

"Well...is there anything else we have to do before we go home?" David asked, looking at the skies. It had gotten colder since leaving the hospital, and clouds were blowing in. He had the distinct impression that a storm was on the way.

"Nope. Let's go home," Cait replied merrily.

"Thank fucking God," Ellie muttered.

They left the fishing village and began to head towards their home.

...

Sure enough, it began to snow as they started their long trek home.

David shivered and complained occasionally as they walked alongside the river. He kept a close eye on the frigid waters, watching snowflakes hit it and disappear in an instant, and wondered if it would freeze over.

"So what's up with Ruby?" Jennifer asked as they walked. "She seems kinda..."

"Cold? Distant? Weird?" Cait asked.

"Yeah. I mean, I don't want to be rude, I don't have a problem with her, I'm just...curious."

"No, I get it. She's always been like that, at least as long as I've known her. I think she's just a really...pragmatic person. She seems to value logic and efficiency over emotions. She kind of cuts to the chase in everything she does, you know?"

"Is it by choice or just the way she is?" David asked.

"You know, I'm not sure. She's a very effective person. We've gone on a few jobs together," Ellie said. "She's *killer* with her sniper rifle. Like, brutally effective. I saw her take down a dozen guys in maybe half a minute."

"Why's she with the fishermen?" Jennifer asked.

"I'm not really sure. I think her family member or friend or...lover? Not sure, they were with the fisherman? Actually, fuck, I have no idea," Ellie replied.

"Think she'd fuck us? Has she ever fucked you?" Cait asked.

"No. Sex has never come up, and I've never seen her fuck, or heard her fuck, or spoke to anyone that fucked her. Maybe she doesn't care about sex," Ellie replied.

"Wouldn't that be nice," Jennifer murmured.

"You think?" David asked.

"I mean, yeah. If I didn't *care* that I never got laid after I became a wraith, it would have made my life a lot happier. Well...a lot less miserable at least. You were talking about sexual isolation. I know what you mean, probably better than you do. I mean, not to take away from whatever you went through, but..."

"No, I get it. I'd have it way worse if I was a wraith." He stepped closer to her and slipped an arm around her waist, holding her to him, and she immediately pressed herself against him. She was very cold, but he didn't let it bother him.

"Being a wraith sucks, but it sucks a lot less if you have the right people in your life, I'm remembering," she murmured.

"You can have us in your life, you know," Ellie said. "I mean, more than we are now. This doesn't have to stop."

"I guess not," Jennifer replied. She was silent for a few moments, then she sighed. "I don't know. I'm...not the most stable person. Becoming a wraith fucked me up, and I wasn't all that great before. So...I'm happy with where this is going for now."

"Okay. Don't feel pressured to do anything," David said, and kissed the side of her head. She smiled and hugged him to her as they walked.

"You're so warm," she murmured.

"I don't *feel* warm out here," he replied.

"Oh...God, I must be *freezing*. I'm sorry," she said, and began to let go of him.

"No, it's fine. Stay, if you want. I want you to," he replied, and, after a few seconds, she stepped closer to him again and let him hold her as they walked along the path.

Cait glanced back at them with a smile on her face and a surprisingly powerful look of...adoration? Affection? He just smiled back at her, unsure of what else to do. He was used to her looking at him like that sometimes, but it was the intensity of it that caught him off guard. He began wondering again what was up with her, but shut it down.

He was too tired to play this mental game again.

Instead, they walked on.

...

David's heart nearly burst out of his chest when he heard the first spray of automatic gunfire coming from ahead of them. They were maybe three hundred feet shy of the campgrounds. It had begun to snow during the last quarter mile, and he knew it was going to get worse. But apparently everything had just gotten worse in a far different manner.

Letting go of Jennifer, he pulled out his pistol and began hurrying forward. Ellie and Cait had already dashed ahead, disappearing into the trees. None of them spoke as they listened to more guns open up, mostly pistols, but he heard a shotgun in there, and maybe two automatic weapons. One he recognized as the rattle of the submachine gun he'd found a few weeks ago. Thank fucking God he'd left it behind, apparently.

Pistol in hand, fearing the worst, listening to shouts and gunfire, David joined Cait at the treeline surrounding the campgrounds. Ellie was somewhere off to the left, a blue blur. They crouched by the trees as Jennifer joined them. Over a dozen men in grubby winter gear were mounting an assault on the front entrance.

"We have to kill them fast," Cait said, taking aim. "There's too many people in there that could get caught in the crossfire."

"Yep," David agreed as he also took aim.

He, Cait, and Jennifer opened fire. They hit the group from the side, but only about half of them were out in the open. The rest were among the trees north of the camp, peppering it with gunfire. David shot one of the attackers in the side of the head and he dropped to the snow in an instant, his pistol falling from his hands, hitting the ground and going off.

It hit another man in the leg, making him scream and drop to his knees. Cait shot him in the throat and he went down in a spray of blood. Three of the men in the clearing returned fire, one of them holding an assault rifle. David shouted as several bullets seared by him.

Once sliced across his shoulder, through the clothing and biting cruelly into his flesh, and he yelled again, louder, and fell back behind a tree.

"David!" Cait cried.

"I'm fine! Keep shooting!" he snarled, waiting for the blinding pain to subside. He waited for the barrage to let up, then leaned around, aimed in their general direction, and emptied the magazine. They were wild shots, but enough to send the survivors in the opening off running for the protection of the trees.

They seemed to be in an unfortunate stalemate. Although they now had two avenues of fire between David, Cait, and Jennifer, and those in the campgrounds, the thieves had the men now retreating and firing back, and those hidden among the trees. And soon they were all hidden among the trees. They began pounding both positions with gunfire.

David wasn't sure how long it was going to go

on for. He couldn't even see anyone now, at least not clearly, and the pain in his shoulder was awful. It was like someone was holding a fucking lighter to his flesh and he could feel blood seeping out of him.

All around him, bullets rained. He heard someone shout, the voice unfamiliar, and leaned back around the tree he was hiding behind. There! He saw a man standing between two trees, holding an assault rifle. *That's fucking mine,* he thought furiously, and took aim. More gunfire hit the area around him, blasting chunks out of the dead trees and sending up plumes of snow, but he forced himself to focus.

David squeezed the trigger.

The shot was great, taking the man wielding the rifle down as it nailed him right in the eye. He pulled back as another bullet came extremely close to puncturing his chest. Suddenly, someone else shouted, another new voice coming from the direction of the attackers. Then another voice screamed and cut off abruptly.

The gunfire began falling silent, until a gunshot rang out, then two more. What was happening? Had zombies or stalkers been drawn in by their fire?

"Fuck! Kill her! *Kill her!*" someone screamed.

No, something worse had found them.

Ellie.

"Go! Go!" David snapped, rushing the opportunity. He leaned out and opened fire, blasting away at their position. Someone stumbled out of cover and he shot them twice in the back. Cait took another man in the back of the head as he tried to run.

After that, it was a confusing mess as David, Ellie, Cait, and the others gunned down the thieves as they tried to flee in the thickening snowfall. He fired off a few more shots, but then didn't see anyone else, and didn't want to hit Ellie. He quickly checked Cait and Jennifer, found them to be okay, and then went looking for Ellie.

"David, wait! Your shoulder!" Cait cried.

"Check on the others!" he yelled back, heading for the treeline where Ellie had apparently circled around and ambushed the assholes attacking them.

"Ellie?" he asked.

Someone groaned, though it definitely wasn't her. He heard muttering as he carefully drew closer. Then, "No! Wait! Don't!"

A gunshot sounded.

"Ellie?!" he called.

"I'm fine, David," Ellie replied, and he saw her through the trees, standing among several dead bodies. "Help me search them, before the snow covers their weapons and supplies." She paused. "You're bleeding. You're shot. Get inside."

"I'm fine, it's just a graze–" he began, coming towards.

"David, get inside *right now!*" she snarled at him.

He stopped dead in his tracks, staring at her in surprise. "Uh...okay," he replied finally.

"Send a few people to help me with this. Then get your ass taken care of. Hurry. I'll be damned if you catch cold or an infection before our job is done," she said, then crouched by one of the bodies, already beginning to be covered up by the snow.

He nodded, then turned away and began jogging back towards the campgrounds. He was pretty desperate to see if Evie and April and Ashley were okay. He saw several people moving around just beyond the gates, and thankfully he saw no bodies laying on the ground. One of the people moving was especially tall, and he hurried towards her.

"Evie!" he called.

"David! Oh thank fucking God," she said, relief obvious in her voice. He hurried over to her and she hugged him tightly. Then she pulled back and looked down at him. "You're shot!"

"I'm okay," he replied.

"Who's shot!?" someone called.

"I am *fine!*" he snapped back. "Just a graze!"

Ashley appeared at his side, staring at his shoulder. "Shit," she whispered. "That's gotta hurt."

"Yeah," he agreed.

"Come on. We need to get you to April," Evelyn said.

"No, we need to make sure everyone's okay."

"*Go,* we'll deal with that. I promise. I'll come tell you as soon as I know how everyone is," Evelyn replied.

He lingered for a few seconds, looking around. He saw Jim and Amanda, Ashley's parents, Ann, they all looked okay. Shaken, to varying degrees, but okay. God, he hoped that the kids were okay, though he saw Ann making for her house and Ashley's mom making for hers.

He was tempted to go check on the Walsh's, but his shoulder throbbed in agony and he grit his teeth and angrily began making his way towards the main house, where April should be. He hurried across the snowy area and in through the front door, where he saw April in the main room laying out blankets on the floor next to some medical supplies.

"Oh, David," she said, jumping as he came on. "Oh, you're hurt! Come here!" she demanded, and he moved over to her.

"Just a graze, babe," he replied.

She winced as she looked at it. "I need to clean

this. Get your top off. Is anyone else hurt?" she asked.

"I don't think so, but I don't know for sure," he replied.

"Once the shooting died down, I figured I should get ready for injured," she said as he painfully got out of his backpack, then his jacket, then his shirt, then his undershirt. Lots of layers in the winter. He looked at his shoulder.

An ugly furrow had been gouged out of his skin and there was a lot of blood. April studied it too, then made him sit down on one of the blankets she'd laid down. She grabbed some supplies and set to work. "Luckily for you, I've got some local anesthetic. I'm going to numb your shoulder so I can clean in peace," she muttered.

He winced as she stuck him with a needle a few times, and then he didn't feel anything, which was a great relief. He didn't look as she went to work.

"What happened out there?" she murmured.

"I don't know. Cait, Ellie, Jennifer, and I were coming back from our trip when we heard the shooting. Ellie managed to sneak around behind them and break the assault. They're all dead, as far as I know," he replied.

"Jennifer?"

"You remember that wraith I told you about? The one who lives in the woods?"

"The one you made love with," she replied.

"Yes. That one. She's decided to come for a visit."

"To make love again?"

"Yes, and to meet you and Evie and some others, I imagine. And to help with the assault."

"You're very kind," April murmured. Now she was cleaning the wound, and he was very grateful that he couldn't feel it.

"How, exactly?"

"Having sex with Jennifer."

"What?" He glanced at her.

"She's a wraith," April replied, looking surprised. He caught brief sight of his wound, made a face and turned away. April went back to work.

"Having sex with Jennifer is not an act of kindness," David replied. "I had sex with Jennifer, and will again, because she offered and I'm attracted to her."

"Truly?" she asked.

"Yes. Why is that so hard to believe?"

"I'm sorry. I'm not trying to insult either of you. I don't mean to imply that I think it's impossible to be genuinely attracted to a wraith, it's just...the way I've heard people talk about them, especially humans, so many of them have been so utterly repulsed by the idea, so disgusted by the mere thought of it, that I *do* find it a bit strange for someone to be naturally attracted to a wraith. I suppose...you can't make yourself be attracted to someone, can you?"

"You really can't," he murmured. "I don't know. I don't want to shit on people who think wraiths are ugly, because I do think you can't control who you're attracted to, but I don't think that means you need to *tell* them you think they're repulsive. At the most, a person might find themselves in a position to turn down a wraith's advances, which can be done without being cruel. But no, to be clear, I *really* want to fuck Jennifer. I think she's really hot."

"I'm glad. She sounds nice." She sealed a bandage carefully over his wounded shoulder and smoothed it gently into place. "Okay, I'm done. You need to move very little for the next several days," she said, sitting back.

"That's not happening," David muttered.

She sighed. "I know. But at *least* not today. And I'll need to check it every day. Multiple times a day in the beginning. If possible, you really should go lay down."

He began to tell her that was out of the question, but then he yawned as a wave of sleepiness washed over him. "Shit, maybe," he muttered. "But I've got so much to do..." he groaned.

"I'll be right back," April said.

"Where are you going?"

"To check on the others."

He nodded, then laid back carefully on the blanket, staring up at the chipped, old ceiling, listening to the sounds of the others moving outside. It didn't sound panicked, at least. He'd heard crying, earlier, one of the children, but now that had stopped. He felt so guilty to subject them to this, but...what was the alternative?

Leave? Were there safer places around?

Maybe the farm, but it wasn't like they were looking for new roommates. Same with the military outpost. Obviously the fishing villages weren't really safe. No, the only real option was to remove the threat.

Or at least the most obvious threat, not like they could remove all the undead. At best, they might be able to remove a few trouble spots with a lot of effort, and make some secure zones. Maybe. But that was always a tenuous prospect.

He heard footsteps coming, Evie's and someone else's, and a moment later, Evie and Cait walked into the room, all smiles and smirks.

"What's going on?" he asked. "Is everyone

okay? Are *you* okay?"

"We're fine, David. Everyone's fine. You were the only one injured. We got lucky," Evelyn replied as she came up to him. She crouched by his side, and Cait stood on his other side, both looking down at him. "Amanda caught them while they were trying to mount an attack and sounded the alarm. I happened to be heading out with Jim to do some poaching, so we had guns. You showed up almost immediately after the attack began. We got very lucky. The children are shaken, but okay. Don't worry, babe, you did great."

"Thank fucking God," he muttered, relaxing.

"Yes. Now, April tells us you need some bed rest, and you're being a little stubborn about it. So we decided we're going to help you with it," Cait said.

"Help me how?" he asked.

"You'll see," Evelyn replied.

She knelt and then scooped him up in her arms, and he let out a surprised sound. "Wow, you are so fucking strong," he muttered as she raised him swiftly off the floor.

"Yep," she agreed.

Cait gathered his stuff and they walked upstairs. David had another strong sense of dreamlike quality sweep over him as he was carried up two flights of stairs, the notion only enhanced by the fact that he was so tired. Evelyn smiled down at him from time to time as she carried him, and he found himself smiling back up at her.

Being carried by her felt...so good. It wasn't the first time she'd carried him, but each time he worried it might make him feel...bad, somehow. He supposed the most obvious emotion would be emasculation, but it never came. It was less that he felt he should feel bad or weak or whatever about being carried by his girlfriend, and more that the society he'd grown up in had kind of programmed him to feel that way.

But maybe he was changing, because it didn't come. Maybe it was easier to stop giving a shit about stupid things when your life was at risk all the time and a lot of people were counting on you. Well, if so, that would be a nice side effect. As she brought him up to their bed, she paused as she stood beside it, an interested look on her face.

"What?" he asked.

"There's something I've always wanted to try with you...Cait, get his cock out," she said.

"Yes, ma'am," Cait replied, setting his stuff down and coming over.

"What are you doing?" he asked.

"You'll see," Evelyn replied with a very sultry smirk that she seemed to have picked up from Cait and Ellie. Cait undid his pants and dug his cock out, which was already rigid because he kept getting hard-ons whenever he touched one of his girlfriends for more than a moment. As soon as it was out, Evelyn lifted him up higher, then slipped it into her mouth.

"Oh my fucking...holy fucking shit, Evie," he groaned as she began sucking him off.

Now *this* was fucking unreal.

She held him firmly and securely, and she didn't bob her head this time as she gave him oral, she lifted him up and down while keeping her head in place.

"*Wow,* this is just...amazingly erotic," Cait whispered.

"Yes. It is. Fuck. Holy shit, Evie," he panted.

He stared at her large head, at his cock disappearing into her big mouth, her lips, luscious and wet, wrapped around it. He could feel her hands beneath him, lifting him with relative ease it seemed, and this was definitely one of those instances where the nature of the situation had a direct increase on the pleasure.

He liked blowjobs, a *lot*, obviously, but this felt even better than a normal one would simply because of how heavily her size was emphasized. David had always known he'd had a thing for women who were taller than him, but dear fucking lord, this was just amazing.

The pleasure was eating into him, consuming him whole, radiating out from his cock as her wonderful lips slid slowly up and down.

She sucked him off like that for another half minute or so, then she took it out of her mouth and grinned down at him. "Okay, now I'm going to lay you down, and Cait and I are going to convince you to take a nap," she said, and began laying him down on their bed.

"I've got shit to do," he complained.

"No, David. You've done enough. All three of your girlfriends are agreed on this one."

"Oh. Well then I guess I'm fucked," he replied.

Cait giggled. "Yes, you are."

As he finished laying down, Cait pulled his pants and boxers off and tossed them away. She began to kiss him, lavishing him with wonderful, long, hot kisses as Evelyn resumed sucking his dick. He groaned into the kisses and pulled her shirt up until her huge breasts had been freed.

They continued making out as more oral pleasure burned into him, engulfing and consuming him. He could feel himself throbbing, pulsing in response to it. Especially when Cait stopped kissing him, took off her shirt, and then joined Evelyn.

"Oh my fucking God, you two are the best..." he

moaned loudly as they both started to drag their tongues across the head of his cock.

He felt powerless before them, watching both of them as they started taking turns putting his cock in their mouth. Cait took it into hers and locked eyes with him as she bobbed her head. There seemed to be a new intensity in her gaze, he saw, or maybe that was just his exhaustion, or imagination. Either way, he liked it.

She was running her hand lovingly up and down his leg as she bobbed her head and her touch was soft and warm and wonderful. They passed him back and forth like that until he started letting off in Cait's mouth. He cried out in primal bliss as his orgasm erupted and he shot his load into her willing mouth. She kept on sucking, staring at him with her beautiful eyes the whole time.

Hot, rapturous ecstasy blasted through him, destroying any hopes he had of staying awake. It was almost like what little energy he had left was leaving through his cock. Cait sucked him dry and then swallowed.

"You doing okay there, handsome?" Evie asked.

"Uh-huh," he managed, his lids heavy.

"Oh yeah, he's not going anywhere," Cait said. "Come on, David, let's get you covered up so you can catch some sleep."

"All right," he murmured.

He got under the blankets and fell asleep almost immediately.

CHAPTER TEN

When he came to, he heard voices talking, though they weren't nearby.

And there was someone in the bed with him, someone warm and curvy that he had apparently wrapped himself around in his sleep. He ran his hands slowly over her body, and surmised that it must be Cait.

Her skin wasn't scaly nor furry, so it wasn't April or Ellie, too small to be Evie, and too buxom to be Ashley. As he shifted around, he confirmed that it was indeed his redheaded lover in the soft moonlight that came in through the windows.

After a little bit, David realized that he was starving, and that his shoulder hurt. A lot. Carefully, he sat up and began to get out of bed.

"Where do you think *you're* going?" Cait murmured.

"To eat," he replied. "I smell dinner...and I've been asleep for too long."

"It's only been an hour or two...I think," she replied, rolling over to face him. "I need to look at your bandage."

"Think I reopened the wound in my sleep?" he asked.

"It's possible. But it wasn't done bleeding by the time April finished patching it," she replied. "Stay here, babe."

She got up, and he got a good look at her ass in the moonlight. There were a lot of things to love about Cait, but he had a particular love of her fat white ass. She returned a moment later with some medical supplies and a battery-powered lantern, then sat on the bed beside him.

She considered him for a moment, then set the supplies down, pulled on some panties, pulled a chair over, and sat down in it. "Sit here," she motioning in front of her on the bed.

He did and she carefully began to peel away the bandage April had laid into place several hours ago. It was stained with blood. "It's stopped bleeding," she murmured, setting the bandage aside. "This is gonna hurt."

He hissed in pain as she cleaned the wound again but otherwise held his peace. He glanced over at her. Her huge breasts hung down practically in his face and jiggled and swayed with each tiny movement of hers.

"Don't," she murmured.

"What?" he asked.

"Reach for them. I know you want to, and you know I like it when you touch them, but you really need to not move right now."

"I wasn't going to," he said.

"You're a terrible liar. We need to work on that."

He just snorted and fell silent, then began thinking about her, if she was lying to him. She finished cleaning his wound and began bandaging it again. "Cait?"

"Yes, David?"

"Is something wrong?"

"What?" she asked, startled.

"Let me rephrase that. I know something's wrong. Will you tell me what it is?" She was silent, working on his bandage probably with more diligence than was required. He sighed. "If you really, honestly don't want to tell me, then I'll respect that, but if there's something wrong with you, I want to know.

And if there's something wrong between us, I think I deserve to know, given our relationship. And if it's something else, then I want to know, and I want to help."

He waited. She was silent for several seconds, then she finished with his bandage. "David...something's happened. A...change. That I wasn't expecting. It relates to you, and it impacts, well, everyone in the relationship. I can't pretend it doesn't. However...I need a little more time to...to wrap my head around it. We can discuss it fully after we take on the thieves. Okay?" she asked, almost a little beseechingly, he thought.

He reached out and took her hand. "Okay, Cait."

"Thank you. Very much. And..." she hesitated, looking a little hesitant and perhaps a little guilty now, "I need something from you. I need you to tell me the truth."

"About? I mean, I haven't lied to you yet."

"I know. I just wanted to relay how important it is. How many sexual partners do you have right now? How many women have you had sex with in this region, including one night stands or flings? List them, please," she asked.

"Um..." he wanted to ask her why, but the expression on her face told him it was genuinely important, and he believed that it was important, so instead he considered it. "There's Evie, and April, and you. Ellie and Ashley, obviously. Jennifer. And now Vanessa."

"And that's it? No one else? You're *sure?*" she asked.

He thought for a few more seconds, then nodded. "Yes. I'm sure. There's no one else. At this point, I'd remember," he replied. "Why?"

"It isn't a jealousy thing, don't worry about that. I just...need to know. Is there anyone you intend to become sexually active with in the next...few days?" she asked.

"Fuck, now that's a lot tougher question. I guess...if they offered, I'd have sex with Katya and Ruby...and Lara, that military woman. I'd definitely fuck her...why? What's this about, babe?"

She bit her lower lip, looking sheepishly at him. "I promise I'll tell you tomorrow night. But there's no one else? It *is* important."

"No. Although with the goddamned *eruption* in my apparent sexual popularity that I've been enjoying over the past month, I can't promise that won't change."

"Okay, that's fair. Will you tell me before fucking anyone you haven't already fucked, if the opportunity comes up, *before* you actually have sex with them?" He stared at her for a moment, still baffled by what the fuck it could be. *Obviously* it was related to sex. But how? "I'm sorry, I know I'm being a pain in the ass."

"It's fine," he replied. "I trust you, Cait. I believe you, and I trust that you wouldn't ask this, nor would you keep anything from me, without a good reason. Yes, I'll tell you."

"Thank you, David," she said, and she got down on the bed and hugged him tightly. "Thank you."

After another few seconds, he asked, "Can you at least tell me if it's good or bad?"

She hesitated, then replied, "It's complicated...but I don't think it's bad...if that helps?"

"I guess it does," he murmured. "Well, whatever it is, I'll wait, and try to put it out of my mind."

"I'm sorry to be cryptic, it just...surprised me. A lot."

"It's okay. Whatever it is...I'm here for you."

"I hope you still feel that way after I tell you what it is," Cait murmured.

"You think I won't?"

"I...don't know. And, to be clear," she added quickly, "it's not a judgment on you. This would surprise anyone." She sighed. "Let's get dinner. I'm starving."

"All right, babe." He kissed her, and she kissed him back with passion.

Then they got up and began dressing. He let the worry over her drift from his mind as much as he could as he carefully pulled his clothes on. The pain in his shoulder was a real problem for moving around. He'd never been outright shot before, but, like he kept telling them, this really didn't feel like a serious gunshot wound, because it wasn't.

It was basically a really bad cut or scrape. A good chunk of skin had been gouged out, and that fucking sucked, and it was going to for a little while, but it wasn't the same as what had happened to Evie. Cait waited patiently for him to get dressed, and even helped him get his boots on.

"Don't be embarrassed," she murmured as she finished tying them.

"I'm not, I'm just..." he trailed off, unsure of what to say.

"You are."

"Maybe. It's...you're so fucking badass, and tough, and it's...it's hard to measure up to that, often. You know? It's hard not to feel like I've got to hide every weakness from all of you."

"David," Cait said, looking up at him, "you're

plenty tough. I think you've proved that by now. And tough isn't everything. I don't need you to be a hardass all the time. Sometimes, yes. But seeing you being loving and kind and thoughtful, is just as important to me as seeing you be decisive and tough. I'm with you for several reasons, and 'tough' isn't at the top of the list."

"What *is* at the top of the list?" he asked.

She sighed, considering it.

"Don't tell me it's sex," David said.

"Would that be so bad?" she replied with a small grin.

"I mean, no...not entirely. I just feel like...there should be something more crucial as the foundation of a relationship, you know? I feel like there are too many pieces of shit out there that are good at sex and bad at...everything else that goes into a relationship, but they keep getting relationships and abusing their partners just because they're attractive or charismatic."

"I feel you," she said. "If it helps, I'd rather have a good person who's lousy in bed than a piece of shit who's great in bed. Not that I'm saying you're lousy in bed. With you, I get both. As for what tops the list? You *care* about me, and you *care* about Evie and April and Ellie. And you show it. You put real, genuine effort in to make us all happy. And you aren't doing it just because we're sucking your dick. You're doing it because you like us, and because you think we're worth the effort, and you want to make us happy. And that...is worth a lot. A *lot,* David. I'm seeing that more and more, the longer I spend time around you."

He stared back at her. "I...don't know what to say."

"It's okay, David. You don't have to say anything. That's my point: you say enough with your actions. Keep that up," she said, and she kissed him. Then she stood and, after a few seconds, he stood with her. It occurred to him, as they held hands and walked downstairs, that he had never really quite had a place like this before. Even back when he was with his family, they'd moved around so often that he'd never really found a home. And although he didn't think poorly of the tremendous effort his parents put into raising him and keeping him safe and fed...

It wasn't the same as what he had now.

Now, he felt like he actually...

Belonged.

The feeling only grew as he and Cait walked downstairs and into the dining area where they found Evelyn, Ellie, Jennifer, April, and Ashley.

"Look who made it!" Ashley declared.

"We were just about to come wake you two," Evie said.

"I didn't hear any screaming, so apparently you two didn't fuck," Ellie said. "And yet you've both got that look on your face..."

"This look comes from a loving relationship," Cait replied.

As they sat down at the table, he just barely caught a little tiny bit of subterfuge between Ashley and Cait. Ashley looked at Cait with wide, inquisitive eyes, and Cait gave the barest shake of her head. Whatever it was, whatever was going on, Ashley knew, and Cait was indicating to her that she had yet to tell him.

God*damn*, what *was* it?!

No. He could wait. He trusted Cait to stick to her word. He instead focused on the food as a ravenous hunger overtook him. The others had cooked up a pretty hearty meal of venison and rabbit, with some rabbit and vegetable stew, toast, and a shitload of peaches. David got himself some milk, then piled his plate high with food and dug in. The eating and pleasant conversation and laughter lasted for about twenty or so minutes before the more serious matters that were overshadowing them all finally could be ignored no longer.

"All right, let's get serious," Ellie said, gathering everyone's attention. "We've gone around and talked to everyone we can talk to."

"How'd it go?" Evelyn asked.

"Not as well as I'd have liked, better than I'd hoped," Ellie replied. "At present, the assault force consists of: myself, Cait, David, Evelyn, Jennifer, Vanessa, Ruby, and Lara."

"That's *it?*" Ashley asked.

"Two goliaths, a soldier, and a godlike sniper isn't insignificant," Cait replied.

"I'm guessing Lara must be the soldier?" Evelyn asked.

"Yes," Ellie said. "She's solid. I trust her."

"Okay. So...how many of them are there?" Evelyn replied.

"We're not sure, but I'd guess on the plus side of fifty. Though maybe not after their loss here," Ellie said.

"Fifty?" Ashley asked. "Eight versus *fifty?*"

"And it gets more complicated," Ellie said.

"*How?*" she demanded.

"We can't just mow the place down wholesale. Besides the fact that that could be a useful outpost and there's certainly a lot of useful supplies in there that we don't want to destroy, we can't confirm that there might not be innocents inside. We don't know if they might have prisoners."

"So how the fuck are we going to do this?" Ashley demanded.

"*We* will handle it, while *you* stay here and hold down the fort. When we leave, until we get back," David said, drawing everyone's attention, "I want all the children brought inside, preferably into the basement, as a precaution, as well as the Walsh's. Everyone else, you, your parents, Ann, the Carlson's, if we think we can trust him with a gun, Benjamin, will be armed, and we'll post guards to cover all the ways into this place. And you are to remain until we return. Do you have that?" he asked, staring at her.

She looked like she wanted to argue, somehow, someway, but finally she just nodded and seemed to make herself say, "I have it."

"Good. Thank you, Ashley. You are playing quite a crucial role."

"Yeah, yeah," she muttered.

"What about *our* plan?" Cait asked.

"I've got an idea. We need to draw them out. And we need some subterfuge. I say three teams, and three stages. Team one is Vanessa and Jennifer. There's a cabin about three hundred feet away from the main camp. You two will get to it, kill any hostiles there quietly, and then Jennifer will hide there. Vanessa will launch an assault and be the hook that draws most of them in. She'll hurry back to the cabin and the two of you will hold off the assault.

"Team two is Ruby and Cait. We'll place Ruby in a position to start sniping their asses, drawing more of them off and splitting the bulk of the force. Cait, you're her bodyguard. Team three is the rest of us, myself, David, Lara, Evelyn. We hit the main encampment, kill any bad guys who are still around. David and Lara will see if there are any hostages while Evelyn and I move on and hit them from the back. Once you've checked out the camp, you join us and we mop up any stragglers."

She sat back, looking more than a little pleased with herself.

"It's not a bad plan," Cait murmured.

"Suggestions? Flaws?" Ellie asked, looking around the table.

David considered it as the others started talking, hashing it out, and they spent the next twenty minutes mainly discussing variations of 'what if this goes wrong?', and occasionally presenting another idea. But ultimately, no one had a better idea of a way to achieve all their intended goals. And once they were finished talking about it, Ashley cleared her throat and leaned forward, looking around the table at them all.

"Now that business is out of the way, what's say we tend to pleasure?" she asked, and she looked at David and Jennifer, who sat beside each other. "I was told that the two of you would be making love tonight, and I would *love* to watch, if you're so inclined to let me."

Everyone else at the table looked at them. Ellie looked sympathetic, and perhaps ready to step in on Jennifer's behalf, given how well they knew each other. Jennifer looked surprised and a little caught off guard. She looked at David inquisitively.

"Only if you're comfortable with it. If you want, no one has to watch," he said.

"I'm okay with an audience," she replied after a moment. "I guess...just so long as everyone's really okay with me being a wraith. And it's okay if you aren't into me, I think that's totally fine. I just...want to make sure."

"I'm pretty sure we're all pretty enthused about this," Evelyn said. "Cait? April?"

"Oh, I'm obviously enthused," Cait replied. "I've already had the pleasure once."

"I'm definitely interested," April said quietly. She looked very aroused, not quite able to meet anyone's eyes. "I really want to watch this."

"Obviously I do," Ellie said.

"I think I've made my position clear," Ashley said.

"Okay then," Jennifer replied. "Then, uh...where's the bed?"

"Upstairs," David replied. "Come on."

Several chairs were pushed back and all of them followed the pair up the stairs and into David's and Evelyn's shared bedroom.

"Wow, that is a *big* bed," Jennifer murmured, staring at it.

"Yep. I'm a big lady," Evelyn replied.

"So this is where you and David sleep?" she asked.

"Most nights," David replied. "April has her own room, Cait and Ellie share one. Though more often than not someone ends up not in their own bed. Usually someone will crawl in here and shove me on my back and ride me in the middle of the night."

"That's usually me," Cait said.

"Let's do this," Ashley said impatiently.

"All right. Let's wash up. It's certainly been a long enough day," David replied.

"Yes," Jennifer agreed. "Definitely."

While the others got settled around the room, David and Jennifer walked over to the washbasin and began stripping. "How'd we do for guns?" David asked as he got undressed, careful of his wounded shoulder.

"Good," Ellie replied. "Seven pistols, an automatic rifle, and a shotgun."

"Only nine of them were armed?" he asked.

"No, they were all armed, but the rest of them, all pistols, were so fucked up that we're just going to scrap them for spare parts. Not a decent haul of ammo, though. They used up most of what they had on them trying to take us down."

"Why are they so fucking bad at this and so fucking persistent?" David asked as he finished stripping and began washing.

"I don't know. It's not really unique. There's a lot of groups out there that usually have strength in numbers but almost all of them are shit lousy shots with no discipline, united only by desperation and cruelty," Cait said. "It'll be good to wipe them out."

"Yep," Ellie growled.

David glanced at Jennifer as she finished undressing by taking her panties off. Fuck, she had a nice body. Still pretty trim and fit. She didn't seem too...corpse-y, for a wraith. The most obvious thing about her was her dead pale skin, her blackened veins across her whole body, and her generally unhealthy appearance. But if you could get past that...she had a nice body.

Nice breasts, great ass, still decently fit. From what he understood, no two wraiths were alike. Some still needed to eat and drink, some didn't. Some decayed, some didn't. Some went bald, some lost limbs, some couldn't talk. It seemed pretty random.

But Jennifer looked good. Slim, trim, skinny really, almost as skinny as April, but a little more filled out than her.

She looked at him anxiously as they washed up together. "I'm still a little cold," she said. "Sorry."

"It's fine." He reached out and laid a hand on her back. She *was* kind of clammy, but it wouldn't stop him.

"David," April said as they finished washing up and began to dry. He glanced at her. "Be careful. Don't move too much, okay?"

"I'll ride him," Jennifer said.

"Probably for the best," he replied after a few seconds. His shoulder was bugging him. Although orgasming would help with the pain, at least.

As they finished drying, the pair of them moved over to the bed and climbed into it. Jennifer seemed careful as they settled down beside each other and began to touch. He ran his hand across her slim, pale body, and felt her own cool hands sliding across his bare skin. She seemed eager and happy simply to touch him, and he couldn't blame her.

Before they had made love that first time, how long had she been alone? She made it sound like it had been a very long time since she'd last been intimate. He knew how she felt, to a certain degree. And now she had him and, apparently, Vanessa. He would *love* to get them together in a threesome.

Preferably a foursome with Katya. She was so fucking hot, too.

It wasn't long before Jennifer leaned in and pressed her lips to his. He kissed her back, pulling her closer to him, running his hand along her hip, her thigh, back up to her tight ass, up the curve of her back. She shivered at his touch and moaned into the kiss, her own hand exploring across his flesh.

"Mmm," she moaned. "You're so...oh...so

warm..." she whispered between kisses. "So *hot,* David. Everything about you is hot..." she moaned, then pressed herself completely against him and moaned louder.

As they kissed, his hand found its way down in between her thighs, and she let out a loud moan and shuddered violently as his fingertip came in contact with her clit.

"Oh *yes.* I fucking *remember* this..." she moaned as he began to massage it.

"I'll bet," he murmured.

"I'll-ah!-I'll try not to-*oh fuck!*-give you a black eye this time," she whispered.

He laughed. "I'd appreciate it."

Ashley laughed loudly. "I'd forgotten about that!"

He heard a few of the other women chuckle as well. They resumed kissing as he fingered her, first massaging her clit, starting out harder than he would have normally, given the fact that she was a wraith. It seemed to be working.

He knew he'd have to work extra hard to get her to orgasm, something he fully intended to do, but this time he was going to be using more than just his hand. They made out and he fingered her for a good five minutes, alternating between rubbing her clit and fucking her with his finger, pushing up repeatedly into that wonderfully sensitive spot of hers, making her hips buck and listening to her cry out in pleasure.

And then he stopped kissing and fingering her.

"What?" she asked, startled. "Are you okay?"

"I'm fine," he replied. "I'm moving onto the next part."

"The sex? We'll need to find some lube..."

"No, Jennifer. That's the part after this part."

"Oh...what then?"

"Spread your legs," he replied.

She opened her legs for him and watched as he got down in between them. "Oh!" she said as it seemed to hit her. "Oh, you don't have to...oh wow," she whispered.

"I want to," he replied. "Though..."

"Yes?"

"I know how loud you get. Although this place is decently soundproofed...I think...we *do* have families here..."

"Oh! Yes, of course. I'll, uh, I'll try to keep it down," she said.

"Good luck with that, he's got a golden fucking tongue," Cait muttered.

"Oh God yes he does," Evie said.

"Yeah...pretty sure my parents have heard me screaming your name when you put that tongue to use," Ashley admitted.

"How fucking awkward that must be," Ellie muttered.

David got to work then, gently parting the lips of her pussy and beginning to lick with firm strokes. Jennifer let out a loud moan and then put a hand over her mouth. She stared at him with wide eyes as he started to eat her out.

He thought she might taste bad or weird or...something, but she didn't. She didn't taste of anything, except maybe a very faint taste similar to what he experienced when he went down on the other women.

For the next ten minutes or so he listened to her moan and cry out and carry on and shout, all from behind her hand, and then both hands as she desperately tried to keep quiet. Her legs spread wide open and her hips bucked and jerked occasionally as he tongued her clit. She got especially noisy when he also began fingering her again.

Before long, between her frantic cries of pleasure, he became aware of heavy breathing from all around him, and then, quiet moans as well. He realized that some of the women must be pleasuring themselves, masturbating to this display. That only made him a hell of a lot hornier and he was looking forward to Jennifer riding his cock like crazy. But he had to make her come first, he had to.

And he did.

It seemed to take forever, and he was literally seconds away from being forced to take a break because between his shoulder and the strain on his fingers, wrist, tongue, and jaw, it was becoming too much, and finally she let out an exultant cry of total, pure, absolute sexual release as she began to orgasm furiously. He pleasured her throughout it, finding a final burst of strength, and barely managed to outlast her as she screamed and cried out and jerked and twitched and spasmed as the climax surged through her body.

It was a wonderful experience.

When she was finished, she let go of him, (she'd been grabbing his hair with one of her hands, the other still over her mouth), and looked down at him with wide eyes. "Okay," she said, "okay, David...now it's your turn. Get on your back."

"Yes, ma'am," he replied.

"Where's your lube?" she muttered as she started looking around.

"Headboard, right there," David said, pointing to their headboard, which they had built several compartments into. They contained a lot of different items, among them lube, given how often April showed up, wanting to fuck.

"Got it," she said, snagging the bottle, opening it, and getting some into her hand. She tossed it aside and began to massage his rigid cock, making him shudder in response. "You made me come so fucking hard," she said, almost growled, staring at him with her bloodshot eyes, "now I'm going to make you fucking come so fucking hard."

He wasn't sure what to say to that, and she apparently wasn't interested in waiting for an answer, because she quickly mounted him, slipped his cock into her pussy, and lowered herself, taking his whole rock-hard length into her.

"Oh *fuck...*" he moaned loudly.

"Big benefit of being skinny, I've found: *super* tight pussy," she murmured.

"Yep," April said.

"Mmm-hmm," Ashley agreed.

"And thank fucking God I got to keep that aspect when I turned," Jennifer said as she began to ride him. "Because you feel *so* big and *so* fucking good in there right now..."

"Yes. Fucking...god*damn!*" he moaned as she began to go faster.

"Remember, don't go for too long," April said.

"I know. I'll make him come," Jennifer replied.

"Aw, come on," he groaned. "I can handle this."

"Don't be difficult, David," Ellie said. "You need to be in as good a shape as you can manage for tomorrow night. You need to rest that shoulder, let it heal as much as possible, because you're almost certainly going to fuck it up during the assault."

"Ugh...yeah, fine," he replied, but it was hard to be annoyed when a tight as fucking hell wraith was bouncing on your dick.

She was fucking tight and he was enjoying the hell out of it. He stared up at her limber, lean body, taking in all her nude beauty as she rode him. And she did look beautiful, vibrant, amazingly sexy, not just because she was naked and fucking him, but because she looked so happy, so enthusiastic as she did so.

She looked like she'd tossed away any and all of her concerns, like she'd forgotten everything that troubled her, like she was among people that she trusted and liked. And honestly, that was the best part of their sexual encounter.

Although how downright *good* it felt was pretty great, too.

He watched her high, firm breasts bouncing with the rest of her as she enthusiastically bounced on his dick, taking the whole thing into her again and again, putting her firm, tight thighs and smooth hips to good use.

And she made good on her word.

Before long, he felt a powerful orgasm rising in him, as though being drawn out by her and her wonderful body and vivacious lust as she stared at him and rode him and reached out, grabbing his hands and holding them up between them both, lacing their fingers together.

"Do it," she whispered, "I can feel it, you're going to come soon. I can just fucking feel it, I can see it on your face, David. Do it. Come in me. I want you to," she panted.

"Oh, fuck, Jennifer...you are *really* good at this," he groaned.

"That's right," she said with a broad grin. "I remember how to do this. You fucking earned this, David. Now fill me up with everything you've got."

She began to go harder and faster, slipping that fantastically tight vagina up and down his cock, clenching it even more tightly around him, and he cried out and began to come within another ten seconds.

"Oh *yes!*" Jennifer cried as he thrust up into her as the first of his seed burst out of him, spraying into her.

More immediately followed as hot pulses of blinding pleasure raced through him, radiating out from the core of his body, filling him as he filled her. His seed left him in hard spurts, pumping her sweet wraith pussy full, and he groaned and cried out, his whole body spasming in pure pleasure as the orgasm overrode everything.

He came until there was nothing left to give.

And then he was spent, left panting and slack against the bed, his shoulder aching faintly from the exertion.

"There," Jennifer murmured, gently patting his sweat-slicked, bare chest, "now rest up, David. We've got a lot to do tomorrow."

"Yeah," he replied, then yawned. "Fuck, I had a nap like an hour ago."

"And you're still tired," Ellie replied. "What's it gonna take to make you sleep?"

"Company," he answered.

"This bed's pretty big..." Evelyn murmured.

"Think we could all fit?" Cait asked.

"If we dragged another mattress in here and set it next to the bed, yeah," Evelyn replied.

"I volunteer mine. Let's do a sleepover, all of us," April said immediately.

"Okay. Be right back," Evelyn said, and left the room.

"Wow, are we really doing this?" Jennifer asked.

"If you want to," David replied.

"I want to. I'm just...I'm still getting used to sharing a bed with someone," Jennifer replied. "Lemme go wash up."

She got up off of him and as she did, Ellie and Ashley both quickly shed their clothes. Evelyn returned a moment later with April's mattress, blankets and all, and set it down next to their bed, right up against it.

"We can share this mattress," Cait said, walking up behind April and hugging her from the back.

"That sounds very nice," April replied.

It wasn't long before everyone stripped and settled in beneath the blankets, and that night David found himself sleeping among six naked women.

CHAPTER ELEVEN

The next day first went quickly, then took forever.

David woke not long after sunrise the next morning and found himself passed between first Evie, then Ellie, then Cait, and then April warned them to stop fucking him because he was going to reopen his wound if he kept it up. She ended up washing and re-bandaging the wound again, saying that it seemed to be doing okay for the moment.

It still hurt like fuck, but no worse than last night. At first he woke up full of energy and he washed, dressed, and helped prepare a large breakfast with a lot of enthusiasm. He did the same as he walked around the campgrounds, checking in on everyone. The snow had only let up about an hour before he'd woken and so everything was covered in a crisp layer of powder, and the forest around them was almost totally silent.

He ended up spending the next four hours going over their arsenal with Ellie and Cait, checking over the various weapons, taking them apart, cleaning them, reassembling them. They wanted as few things to go wrong during this whole thing as possible. They had managed to get quite the haul from the thieves' failed attempt.

And, interestingly, he actually ended up managing to claim the assault rifle for himself. Ellie didn't want it, saying it wasn't really the kind of weapon she preferred. Cait liked her shotgun too much. Evelyn couldn't use it, because her fingers were too big. Jennifer didn't seem interested in it.

So he got an assault rifle. He spent a while

cleaning it, taking it apart, cleaning it some more, putting it back together again. He'd learned how to do that over the course of his life. It seemed like a useful skill to have.

It was a solid piece of hardware and took thirty round magazines of nine millimeter ammo, so that was pretty fucking nice, since that was the type of bullet they had most in abundance. He managed to put together four magazines for it, and another four for his pistol. By the time he was done with all that, lunch was ready.

It was after lunch that things began to slow down.

He grabbed a pair of knives and spent a while cleaning and sharpening them, chatting with Ellie and April and Jennifer while he did that. When he was finished, he went and selected his outfit. Something that would protect him from the cold and leave him mobile.

Unfortunately, none of them had the luxury of bulletproof vests. Lara might, though, he figured. As he was preparing his outfit, figuring out what he was going to bring, something abruptly occurred to him, and he went back down to where the others were preparing their own arsenals still.

"Something just hit me," David said.

"What?" Ellie asked, looking up.

"We should all bring backpacks, any duffel-bags we have, too, all empty. Or as empty as we can make them. Might want to bring *some* emergency food and medical supplies, just in case. But after we hit that camp, I mean, if it all goes the way it's supposed to, there's at least a decent chance that there'll be a haul there. And we can't necessarily trust that it will *stay* there, unless one or two of us wants to hang out and guard it. We'll want to bring back as much as we can, in either scenario."

"Shit, you're right," Cait murmured.

"See what you can rustle up," Ellie said.

And so that's what he'd spent another hour doing, hunting through first all of the main office, then going around to the cabins and asking people for whatever they could spare. In the end, they got enough backpacks for everyone going, and four duffel-bags and two fur sacks that were easy enough to shove into the backpacks.

David had to admit, he wasn't looking forward to the walk back, as he was going to no doubt be loaded down with all manner of heavy gear. After that, he still had a few hours to kill, and time seemed to come to a crawl.

First, he took a shift of guard duty for two hours that he shared first with Jennifer, then with Cait. They took turns standing watch atop one of the cabins and patrolling around the perimeter. Occasionally, they shot a zombie that wandered too close to the property.

The conversation made the time go by more quickly, but they didn't stick together for too long before one of them would go off to patrol. Seconds went by. Minutes went by. Eventually, somehow, David managed to get through his shift and headed back inside.

There was still about an hour and a half before Lara was due to show up.

He wandered around, talking with anyone he could find, but they were all, to varying degrees, in a similar state, and conversation grew difficult.

Finally, after what felt like ages, Lara arrived at the front entrance of the campgrounds just about the time the sun was beginning to set. Amanda, who was on watch, almost shot her, but Lara convinced her to at least confirm her identity by sending someone to check with the people in charge, and so she'd sent Ann off.

David had told everyone to start getting ready and run out to the main gate, where he found her waiting with a submachine gun and her uniform that still looked amazing on her. She looked anxious, but relieved when she saw David.

"It's okay, Amanda. She's a friend," he said.

"All right. I'm sorry, ma'am. We've had several attacks of the human variety just lately," Amanda replied from where she stood atop the nearest cabin.

"It's okay," Lara replied, "I genuinely completely understand."

"Come on. We're preparing to get underway. We've got a plan," David said.

"Good." She followed him into the campgrounds and then into the main office, where all the others were gathered on the first floor, finishing up getting their gear on. They'd already made sure everything they wanted to take was pre-selected and ready for quick access.

"You made it!" Cait said.

"Yes. I almost didn't. I managed to slip away after telling one of the others that I was going out for a supply run to a place I found that I thought might have spare parts for our solar panels," Lara replied. Ellie snorted and looked away. "What?" Lara asked.

"Your boss threatened our life to get those solar panels," David said.

"What? He did?" she asked, looking surprised.

"To be *completely* fair, Ellie threatened him first. Though it wasn't much of a threat," David replied.

"Excuse me?" Ellie asked, looking sharply at

him.

"What I meant was," he replied, holding up his hands, "it was three of us with pistols against fifteen fucking people with goddamned assault rifles and shotguns. Don't get me wrong, I know everything you do is genuine, Ellie, but you aren't fucking insane. That was a no-win situation, so it was a bluff."

She sighed disgustedly and got back to prepping her gear.

"It's still a really sore spot for her," Cait said.

"I'm sorry. I didn't know that. Stern said that they salvaged them from a bunker out in the woods. I didn't realize you were there."

"We were trying to salvage them to help those doctors," David replied. "Or even just salvage *one*. He couldn't even give us one."

"Shit. I'm sorry. He's always been a hardass, but up until the past few months, he was rarely an outright asshole." She sighed and shook her head. "We should probably stay focused. What's the plan?" she asked.

David told her while he suited up with his own gear. He was relieved to see that she agreed with the plan. They were all, to varying degrees, combat-experienced, but Lara was someone who, he figured at least, had real military experience. If she thought the plan was good, then there was probably a better chance that it was actually good. After gearing up, he checked in with Ashley, to make sure she didn't have any further questions or concerns.

"Don't worry, David. I can hold down the fort here. I'll start moving everyone into position as soon as you're gone," she replied. "Just...don't do anything stupid out there and come back to me. All of you fucking better come back."

"We fully intend to," Cait replied.

She gave all of them a hug and a kiss on the mouth, save for Jennifer and Lara, and then they were off, heading into the fading sunlight and the cold.

...

They managed to make it to the hospital without any real trouble, which only made David more nervous as they crept through the fading twilight along the river. There were a lot of things that could go wrong, and every minute that went by seemed to crank up the tension.

He kept expecting a pack of vipers to slink from the waters, a group of stalkers to leap from the trees, a squad of humans to launch an assault from the shadows.

But there was nothing, save for a few zombies that wandered across their path.

They made it to the hospital as the last of the sunlight faded.

David was relieved to see that Ruby was there and Vanessa was already geared up. She'd actually smeared what might have been oil, something dark, across her face. War paint, he realized. She also held what he figured had to be Widowmaker. It was a *big* fucking machine gun, something that would probably take all his strength to lift.

"What the fuck is that?" he asked.

She grinned savagely. "It's called an M Sixty. Old school military weapon, hardcore, packs quite a punch. We are gonna fuck some people up tonight."

"Apparently," he murmured.

Vanessa looked terrifying, more like a warrior goddess than ever now. Ruby wore tight, dark clothing over her vivid red fur and carried a rifle with a high-quality looking scope on it. She was checking it over, sitting on one of the couches. Ellie filled them both in on the plan, which they each were amenable to. Especially Vanessa. She seemed to particularly enjoy the idea of being bait, though Jennifer looked a little anxious.

"Don't worry, Jen. I won't let anything happen to you. I'll be doing most of the fighting. All you have to do is watch my ass. Not literally, don't get distracted. Just make sure no one sneaks in behind us and tries to cap me. You can handle that, right?"

"Yes," Jennifer replied. "I can handle that."

"Good. Like I said, I'll take care of you."

That seemed to make her feel better.

They warned the doctors to be ready to receive casualties, just in case, and though they looked anxious, they assured them that they stood ready to help. Provided any injured made it back to the hospital.

It was a long walk.

And with that, they grabbed the last members of their team, and headed into the darkness.

. . .

They retraced the route that he and Ellie had taken, cutting a path through the darkness and the cold. Despite his previous anxiety, David was actually feeling better now. Maybe it was that they were actually doing this, actually walking directly to where the main event would unfold. Probably it was the fact that they had gathered everyone, and the backup they were receiving was not inconsiderable.

Vanessa looked like a complete fucking badass,

Lara seemed very competent, and there was a stony stoicism to Ruby that seemed to embody that of an exceptionally competent sniper. It was easy to believe what Cait and Ellie had to say about her.

He felt good about this plan.

Although it would be very dangerous, because so much in life was random and luck-based, these were competent people, people he felt he could trust and rely on. And based off of everything he had seen so far out of the thieves, they had more cruelty than brains. His anxiety didn't leave him completely though.

As they broke away from the river and plunged once more into the dark, frozen forest, he couldn't help but think of all the things that could go wrong, all the ways in which they could be hurt, *who* might be hurt. He felt very guilty for knowing that he had preferences. If someone *had* to get hurt, or even killed during this thing…

He didn't even want to think about it.

So instead, he focused on getting his head straight, honing his attention. He was going to need to be ready for this assault, for he played an important part in it. They all did. And not only would he have to watch out for himself and for his friends, but for potential innocents as well.

He could easily envision people being held prisoner here, or, even if not outright prisoners, but not thieves themselves, maybe too afraid to leave. And then, of course, there were zombies, stalkers, and other things to be paranoid of.

Almost certainly they would be drawn in by all the gunfire and shouting.

Eventually, they returned to the same hill overlooking the area that he and Ellie had first arrived at yesterday. Ellie whispered quickly to Ruby and Cait, and then they were off, breaking away to the left to circle around and find a good vantage point that would give them a view of the area in between the cabin and the main encampment.

She then spoke quickly to Vanessa and Jennifer, pointing, and the pair of them nodded and headed off in the opposite direction, making for the cabin. Then she retreated a little bit to join him, Evelyn, and Lara.

"And now, we wait," she whispered. "It should take Ruby and Cait five minutes to get set up, and I told Vanessa to strike after ten minutes if possible. Once she hits, we let everyone possible leave the camp. We'll play it by ear, but I think we should let two minutes go by before we hit the camp. Any questions?"

"No," David said, and Evelyn and Lara shook their heads.

He studied them. Ellie looked fierce, almost like she was looking forward to the battle ahead. Evelyn looked worried but prepared. Lara looked grim and serious. David wondered how he looked.

He ran a hand over the length of the cold metal barrel of his rifle in the darkness, waiting. He double checked the rifle and the pistol, the safeties were off, the weapons were ready for business. So was he. David did not like murder any more than most other people, but over the years he had grown colder towards the idea, bolder, perhaps.

Sometimes, you needed to kill people.

And sometimes, unfortunately, you needed to go out of your way to do so, to prevent them from harming you or yours or anyone else. Time and again these fuckers had proven themselves to not just be assholes, but monsters. In all honesty, David thought that they had sealed their fate the moment they set fire to River View.

How many had died there? Dozens, at least. Over fifty, maybe more. Too many. Way, way too many. And how many others had they murdered before and after that? How many had they robbed and raped?

It was going to stop, and David found that he didn't really feel all that bad about what was about to happen.

The minutes ticked by in the chilled darkness. He and Ellie carefully watched the encampment, studying those who moved around. There seemed to be roughly the same number as last night, which made sense.

Those who attacked the campgrounds would probably have already left by the time they'd come to spy on the group. The atmosphere was different this time, though. Less laughter, more shouting. He saw the man from before, presumably their leader, moving among a group gathered around a fire.

He was angry, yelling.

Probably pissed about yet another failed attempt to attack David's group.

Well, he was about to get a taste of his own medicine.

Suddenly, gunfire sounded. He saw muzzle flare from the east, towards the cabin Vanessa would ultimately run to, and although he couldn't see the woman herself, he knew it had to be her. She was firing into the crowd with a pistol, and he saw several men go down.

They all shouted and scrambled and began returning fire, but Vanessa was already running. She fired over her shoulder a few times to keep their attention. The leader screamed for them to follow, and the general alarm went up. This was actually perfect.

They were all pissed, all angry, all riled up.

It meant that almost all of them would blindly follow her into the forest, intent on murder, whether they realized it or not, they would be seeing this as perhaps some form of revenge for all their failures. Even if they had no idea who was attacking them, they saw it as an opportunity to bleed out all their frustrations and fury.

There was a chaotic and abrupt exodus as over thirty men rushed out into the woods. As the last of them headed off, he heard the crack of a sniper rifle, and more shouts.

"Go!" Ellie snapped, and set off.

They followed after her.

David's heart began hammering even harder in his chest. This was it. Do or die, moment of truth. Ellie took the lead, with Lara behind her, and him and Evelyn bringing up the rear. He could see a few others lingering in the camp, all of them holding weapons, talking loudly to each other, mostly asking each other what the fuck was going on.

David and the others approached as silently as they could, but it was easy to be overlooked given the sheer amount of gunfire going on. He heard more cracking from Ruby's sniper rifle and now the heavy, *heavy* rattle of Vanessa's Widowmaker. It sounded absolutely fucking insane.

And then they struck.

Ellie was the first to open fire, and David squeezed the trigger at almost the same instant. Their shots were excellent, taking two of the armed thieves in the back. Lara struck next, shooting a man in the side of the head, then another in the neck.

Evelyn added her own gunfire to the mix. The survivors screamed and scrambled and returned fire, and for several seconds, it was a chaotic mess. David emptied his assault rifle in a series of careful, controlled bursts, and managed to down four of the survivors.

"Lara, Flank!" Ellie snapped, jerking her finger to the right. She looked at David and Evelyn. "Stay here. Keep the pressure on them."

And then she was gone in the other direction. They knelt among the trees and kept hunting for targets to take down. Somewhere, he heard someone crying, a woman, and was extremely glad that they had thought to not perform wholesale slaughter on the entire encampment. There were roughly half a dozen survivors moving among the buildings now.

One leaned out to fire on his position and Evelyn caught him right as he was doing that, the bullet hitting his forehead. As he fell, David managed to shoot another man three times in the back as he ran between the buildings. He screamed and collapsed to the ground.

David ended his life with another shot to the temple.

One of the men broke and began sprinting into the trees. Unfortunately, he ran right into Lara's position and she shot him in the face.

It didn't take long for them to finish off the remaining thieves left behind at the hunting lodge encampment and move in, like a noose tightening around a neck. David kept a wary eye out as they hurried up to the buildings.

"David, Evie, search. Lara, come on," Ellie said.

The pair ran off, towards the sound of the fighting, preparing to turn the two-pronged assault into a tri-tipped massacre. He and Evelyn got to work. There were almost a dozen buildings, most of them built in a rough square around the central one, the hunting lodge. They were mostly cabins, a few shacks, nothing incredibly significant.

"Watch my back," he whispered as he approached the first one.

"Don't worry, I'm here," Evelyn replied tightly.

He didn't hear crying anymore, though it was hard to hear anything. Although the amount of gunfire had died down, there was still a fair amount of it. He pushed open the door and looked around inside. Someone's bedroom and not much else. The place was a chaotic mess, and he had the impression that several people shared the space.

He quickly checked anywhere someone might be hidden, found no one, and moved on. The next four shacks were like this: disorganized, smelly, empty. On the fifth one, he nearly got stabbed.

As he opened up, someone screamed, and he leaped back, raising his rifle, as someone took a swing at him.

"Wait!" he cried, spying a pair of women in the shack. One was crouching in the corner, and from the tears on her face it was obvious she was the one who had been crying, the other had been waiting near the door, holding a combat knife.

"Back the fuck off!" the knife-wielder screamed.

"Wait, I'm here to help!" David pleaded, lowering his rifle.

"Bull-fucking-shit, just back the fuck off or I'm going to stab you in the fucking throat!"

"Please, just let us go," the second woman moaned, looking almost sick with fear.

"I'm honestly, truly here to help," David said.

"That's why we didn't fire into any of the cabins."

"You just wanted to see if they had any fuck toys around so you and your fucking *boys* could claim us for yourselves," the knife-wielding woman snarled.

"What? No! I'm the only man here and we aren't here to hurt or capture you."

"Fuck you! You fucking liar!"

"Evie?" he said, stepping back.

Evelyn stepped closer and peered in through the door. Both women seemed at first startled by her appearance, and then seemed to relax slightly. "He's telling the truth," she said. "We're really here to help you."

The woman holding the knife stared at them with wide, fearful eyes, then slowly lowered it. "If you are, then let us go. Just let us get our shit and go."

"If that's truly what you want, we won't stop you, but it's *incredibly* dangerous out there right now. This place is infested with stalkers and there's still fighting going on. If you'll just wait here, we can bring you somewhere safe. You don't have to stay there with us, but at least let us get you to safety before you figure out what you want to do," David pleaded.

The woman holding the knife stared at him for several seconds, then glanced back at the other woman, and then back at David and Evelyn. Finally, her shoulders sagged, and in that moment, she looked utterly exhausted. "Fine," she whispered, "fine, we'll stay here. Just...please, *please* don't be lying," she added.

"I know words don't really mean much now, but we aren't. We *will* help you, I promise," David replied.

"Just wait here and lock the door. We'll be back

as soon as we can, we have to finish them off," Evelyn said.

"Okay...thank you," the woman replied. She hurried across the shack and shut and locked the door, and David let out his breath in a long sigh, then looked to the next cabin and began hurrying over to it. They still had a job to do.

"You handled that well," Evelyn said as they searched the next shack.

"Did I?" he replied.

"Yes. I believe you did. Are we going to offer to let them stay with us at the campgrounds?"

"Yes. I want them checked out by the doctors first, to make sure they're okay, and then we'll bring them back with us and offer them one of the cabins. If they aren't interested, then we'll get them a fair amount of supplies and help them however we can."

"Good."

They finished searching the ring of cabins and shacks, and then the main lodge, as quickly as they could. David wasn't sure how much time had passed, but it felt like too long. Although apparently it was just in time, because right as they were gearing up to go, a trio of men in grubby clothing came running into the camp.

"Grab whatever you fucking can, we're getting the fuck out of here!" one of them snapped.

David empty his assault rifle into them, gunning them down as quickly as he could. They waited to see if anyone else showed up, then set off to help the others. The fighting had almost completely died down. David didn't hear the crack of Ruby's rifle nor the heavy chatter of Widowmaker anymore. Just some occasional gunshots at this point.

That could either be good, or bad. A few people

were groaning in pain and someone was asking questions in a panicked voice. None of the voices were familiar. Which could also be a good or a bad thing.

They carefully made their way towards the cabin and listened as the gunshots rang out. At one point, someone burst out of the trees onto the path, an unfamiliar man holding a shotgun. As they all aimed at each other, a gunshot sounded and he pitched forward, falling limply to the ground. Ellie emerged from the same spot he had.

"You're okay," she said.

"Yes. There's two survivors back at the camp, hostages, I'm pretty sure. They've agreed to wait there for us," David replied.

"Okay. Keep going, check on Vanessa and Jennifer. If they're okay, go back to the camp with them and wait there for us. I've told Lara to get back to camp after she runs a few assholes down. I'm going to find Ruby and Cait, and do a little hunting. There's a few left."

"You want any help?" Evelyn asked.

"No, my senses are the best one for it. I think we're going to have stalkers incoming, so get back there right now," Ellie replied, then slipped back into the darkness before either of them could respond. David looked around anxiously.

"Well...shit," Evelyn muttered.

"She's right. Come on," David said, and hurried on.

They continued along the path, finding bodies everywhere. Occasionally, they would stop to grab a discarded gun, usually a pistol, and toss it into their backpacks, but mostly they ran. David could hear groans out there in the trees, and knew that at least zombies had been drawn in. They at least managed to make it to the cabin.

"Hold it! Who the fuck is that?!" Vanessa snarled.

"It's me! It's David and Evie!" David replied, freezing, panic exploding inside of him.

"Fuck, sorry, you two." She was panting. "Fuck," she muttered.

"Are you okay? What's wrong?" David asked.

"Took a few bullets, but I'll be fine. What's happening?" she replied from the broken window she was standing near. The front of the cabin she and Jennifer had occupied was so ridiculously bullet-riddled that it almost looked fake.

"Things are good. Found two survivors. Ellie's okay, Lara's okay, as far as I know. We need to get back to the lodge. Can you make it?" he asked.

"Yeah, I'll be fine. Takes more than a few bullets to immobilize my big ass," Vanessa replied. "Come on, Jen."

A moment later, the front door opened, and David winced. She'd been shot in the leg, the shoulder, and it looked like a bullet had grazed her stomach. Jennifer came out behind her, looking a little shaken, but otherwise all right.

"Come on," Vanessa growled, and hurried off, still toting her huge weapon. They all began making their way back to camp.

"You're okay?" Jennifer asked.

"Yeah, we made it through without a problem. You?" David replied.

"I'm good," Jennifer said. "But Vanessa..."

"I'm *fine*. Seriously," Vanessa grunted.

"She's a fucking force of nature," Jennifer muttered.

"Goddamn right," Vanessa replied.

Something groaned from up ahead, and a dark figure stumbled onto the path. David could see the camp ahead of them. He cursed, raised his pistol, and fired. The zombie dropped. A few seconds later, another figure appeared near one of the buildings.

"Identify yourself!" it demanded. David sighed in relief: it was Lara.

"It's us," he said. "We found Vanessa and Jennifer."

"Shit, thank God," Lara replied, lowering her weapon. She grimaced as they came up to her. "You're hit."

"I'm fine," Vanessa repeated. "We need to fortify this location."

"Yes," David agreed. "Lara, I'm giving you a special job. Come with me. Everyone else, get ready."

They all replied quickly and got to work, and Lara followed him across the camp. "We've got two survivors here. They're scared, but I managed to convince them to let us help. I want you to get in there and make sure nothing happens to them."

"Understood," Lara replied, and he was kind of surprised she didn't argue with him or at least suggest something else, since he was basically giving her a babysitting job.

He thought it might be because she was ex-military, but...no. They only respected actual, real chain of command, and there was no way she would ever confuse him with a member of the military. Either way, it was helpful. He walked over to the cabin in question and knocked on the door.

"It's me, David," he said, then paused. "Uh, I just realized that I never told you my name, but hopefully you remember my voice. Can you open up?"

There was a pause. "Go to the window," came the reply through the door.

He and Lara moved over to the window. The pale, haggard face of the knife-wielding woman appeared. She scrutinized the two of them, then nodded and moved back over to the door. They followed, and she opened up.

"This is Lara, she's with us. She's going to protect you. Zombies are coming, and probably stalkers. Once we regroup and wipe out any undead that show up, we'll raid this place for supplies. If you could help us find any hidden caches or point us to the most useful stuff, that would be extremely appreciated. From there, we'll take you to get checked out by some doctors, and then we'll get you back to our home," David said.

The woman stared at him for a few seconds, suspicion obvious on her face. "What do you want in return?" she asked finally.

"What?" he replied, glancing back over his shoulder as he heard another gunshot.

"As payment," she said, sounding irritated.

"Nothing."

"Nothing. At all. You're fucking bullshitting me," she growled.

"No, we're not," Lara said. "I need to come in now."

"Fine," she said, and stepped back, making room.

"I'll keep this building secure," she said. David nodded tightly and she closed and locked the door once more. He rejoined Evelyn and the others. They were searching bodies, grabbing whatever ammo they could. David checked his. He'd burned through two magazines for the rifle, so not too bad. So far, at least. All around him, he could hear groaning, and suddenly wondered if the assault had been the easy part.

They all tensed as they heard footfalls, drawing closer.

"Who's there?!" Vanessa snapped.

"It's us!" Cait said. "We're coming in."

Cait, Ruby, and Ellie emerged a moment later from between two of the shacks. Ruby was limping and had a hand thrown over her shoulder, though her face was calm. He saw a bandage wrapped tightly around her right thigh. It was bloody.

"What happened?" he asked.

"Some fucking bodyguard I turned out to be," Cait muttered.

"They were stray bullets, there was nothing you could have done," Ruby replied. To David, she said, "I was hit twice, but the bullets went through cleanly and no major arteries were hit. I'll be fine. I have a high pain threshold. Is that building secure?" she asked, pointing to the hunting lodge.

"Last I checked, but that could have changed by now," he replied.

"I intend to go up into the second story and provide cover fire," she said.

"Fine. Cait, go with her," David replied.

"On it," Cait said, and they headed off towards the central structure.

"What's it like out there?" David asked, looking at Ellie.

"Not good. It's hard to tell, but there's at least a shitload of zombies coming in, and a lot of stalkers, I think. And–" She froze as something rustled nearby. "Fuck, get ready!" she snapped.

A second later, a stalker burst from between two of the buildings and came shrieking for them. Ellie snapped off a shot, taking it right between the eyes. A general roar went up, seemingly all around them, and then the battle recommenced.

It was chaos.

Stalkers seemed to come from everywhere, in between every building, over the buildings, from every shadow. There were a dozen of them, two dozen. David immediately opened fire, spraying a trio of them as they approached, careful to remember where the shack containing Lara and the two survivors was.

He put the stalkers down, shifted aim, shot another three times in the chest, then aimed higher and popped two zombie skulls as they began stumbling out of the forest towards the encampment.

This was looking bad.

Didn't matter. They only had a single choice and that was fucking fight for their lives. David emptied his assault rifle putting down another half dozen zombies and a pair of stalkers. He quickly reloaded and kept firing. Overhead, he heard two guns going off: Ruby's rifle and, presumably, Cait's pistol.

Beside and behind him, Evelyn, Vanessa, Jennifer, and Ellie opened fire with everything they had. Bullets flew, undead bodies fell, blood splashed onto the buildings and the ground and pretty much everywhere.

David didn't know how long he spent mowing down zombies and stalkers as they popped up, but it felt like way, way too long. He soon ran out of ammo for his assault rifle and dropped it almost without thinking about it. In one smooth motion he pulled out his pistol and resumed fire. Despite everything, all his fears and anxiety, he felt clear and smooth and so in the moment.

During that battle, he actually felt the weeks,

months, and years of practice he'd had at surviving and fighting and shooting undead monsters.

He wouldn't say he felt *good*, but he felt competent and alive and fucking wired, and that was pretty close to good.

Though he faltered as he reached for what he realized was his last magazine and slipped it into the pistol. How many of these fucking things were there?! There were so many bodies. He'd probably killed three dozen so far, and who knew how many the others had killed. More zombies were coming, at least they were easy to deal with. He raised his pistol once more and opened fire. One down, two down, three, four…

Five. And then he didn't see any more.

David waited, and listened as the others slowly stopped firing, and a long silence settled over the hunting lodge encampment.

After a solid minute, Jennifer said, "Is it over?"

"I think so," Ellie muttered. She let out a long sigh. "Or at least it's the eye of the storm. Come on, people! Let's grab what we can while we've got this chance!"

David took several deep breaths and let them out, trembling now as the adrenaline high passed, and watched his breath foam on the air.

Then he got to work.

EPILOGUE

David sat in an armchair on the ground floor of the main office and felt content.

And fucking exhausted.

They'd done it. They'd actually managed to pull it off. He drained the rest of his water and watched everyone in the room and thought back. It was hard to believe it had been just three hours since finishing off the last of the zombies. It felt like three fucking days given all they'd had to do. Fifteen minutes was all they had been willing to spare gathering supplies from the hunting grounds.

The two women who they'd found and had agreed to help, Chloe and Lena, were very helpful, and pointed them towards a large stash of food and another stash of guns and ammo. They also agreed to carry their own load. And so they'd gathered.

After packing as much as they could, they'd finally decided to get out of there after having to kill first the occasional stray zombie, then a stalker, then several zombies that showed up in a group. They booked it out of the hunting grounds and began making their way back to the hospital.

The trek seemed to take forever, partially because they had wounded, partially because they kept running into zombies and the occasionally stalker. But they did make it back, and the doctors were ready for them, and they immediately set to work patching up Ruby and Vanessa. They checked over the others, and patched up a few scrapes and cuts, and took a look at David's shoulder. In all the chaos, his wound had reopened and he'd bled a fair amount.

Vanessa had told them she'd catch up with them later, after she had a few days to rest, and Ruby opted to spend the night at the hospital. They agreed to let each woman keep the haul she'd gathered as payment for helping out, and then the rest of them had thanked them once more, bid them goodnight, and headed off again.

The walk back to the campgrounds seemed to take even longer. Everyone was tense, afraid of some new threat that might attack them now that they were so close to home. Like tripping at the finish line. But no, they made it to the finish line and beyond. As they drew closer, Chloe and Lena spoke a little with Cait and Evelyn.

Mainly they asked questions about where they were going. They seemed to relax bit by bit as they drew closer to the campgrounds. When they had finally returned, he found Ashley waiting for him with a shotgun by the front entrance. The look of relief and happiness on her face was more than a wonderful welcome home. She had hugged and kissed him, then Cait, then Evelyn and Ellie.

From there, they had dropped everything off upstairs to be sorted out later and let everyone know that everything was okay, it had gone about as well as could be expected. And, naturally, Ashley suggested they have a party.

So they'd thrown a party.

Booze was broken out, big meals were cooked, and people had been coming and going all night long. David had talked with just about everyone and eventually he'd become so exhausted that he needed to just sit down and re-hydrate.

Jennifer and Lara had opted to at least spend the night, because trying to go home in the middle of the frozen night after all this was something neither of them wanted to do. And they seemed to be mixing and mingling pretty well. Some people seemed a little wary of Jennifer, but no one was rude to her, as far as he'd been able to tell.

Lara had come to talk to him for almost forty minutes, mostly asking him about himself. If he didn't know better, he'd say she was enamored with him, but that seemed unlikely. She had to be a good decade older than him, plus she was ex-military with no doubt very high standards.

Then again, maybe he was wrong.

Right now, he looked out across the group of people hanging out in the main room of the ground floor, and he spied Lara talking with Cait. They were having what appeared to be a rather serious discussion. Cait asked Lara a question, he thought. Lara shook her head firmly, like she was very certain of her answer as she replied, and Cait looked...relieved? Grateful? He wasn't sure. Lara asked a question. Cait adopted a small, almost shy smile and nodded. Lara's eyes widened and she smiled and touched her arm.

What were they talking about?

He realized that Cait still needed to tell him her secret, but then she looked over at him, caught his eyes, and smiled sweetly at him. She said something to Lara, who looked over at him as well. She, too, smiled, but it was very shy.

Surprisingly shy. It didn't fit the calm, smooth, at times grim competence that he'd seen her display tonight. She looked back at Cait uncertainly, and she said something that he thought was encouraging, and nodded, and gave Lara a tiny push in his direction, then smirked at him and watched her cross the room.

He sat up straighter, deeply curious now.

She came to stand before him.

"Hi, David," she said evenly.

"Hello, Lara. You did really well out there tonight," he replied.

"Thanks," she murmured. She hesitated, opened her mouth to say something, then cleared her throat and looked embarrassed. "Could I speak with you? Uh...alone? Upstairs?"

"Uh...yeah. What about?" he replied, standing.

"It's personal," she whispered.

"All right. Although first I need to speak to Cait about something," he replied.

"Wait," she said, reaching out and grabbing his wrist. He glanced down, and she quickly let go of him. "Sorry...um...Cait told me that the, uh...the thing you need to talk about, it can wait until after we...talk."

"Oh. Well, all right then."

He'd waited this long, and he was really interested to see what Lara had to say. As he began making his way for the stairs, he saw that Ellie and Evie had joined Cait. Cait was whispering in Ellie's ear, and when she finished, Ellie flashed him a fierce grin, as did Evie. What the fuck did they know that he didn't?

He supposed he'd find out in a few minutes.

"My room's at the top," he said, and led her up. The way was lit mostly by moonlight, and a few candles they left out in the hallways some nights. He got them up to his bedroom and lit a few candles, then pulled back one of the curtains to let more moonlight in. It was bright tonight, reflecting off all the snow.

"So, what's up?" he asked, looking at her.

She lingered in the doorway, looking uncertain,

which, again, looked so alien on her. She was still wearing her uniform, and he still thought it looked so fucking sexy. She stepped inside and closed the door behind her.

"Well, um, first of all, I wanted to say you did very well out there. I was very impressed," she said.

"Thank you. Same to you, although I figured you were going to do great."

"Thanks," she murmured. She looked around the room, her eyes darting to and fro. She cleared her throat twice.

"Lara," he said. "Whatever it is, whatever you want to talk about, you can just...talk to me. I'm very easy to get along with. You'd have to say something pretty overtly awful to get a bad reaction out of me."

She laughed softly. "I suppose so. You're...quite an anomaly, I must admit. I was so confused tonight. About your relationships, I mean. I could tell there was something between you and Cait the first time we met. Just the way she looked at you. But it also seemed like there was something there with you and Jennifer, though that was less certain. Then I saw the way you were with Evelyn. And the way Ashley kissed you...I've spoken to almost everyone here, during the party, so I have a much clearer picture now. I must admit, I didn't exactly expect a warm reception. I know my group has done much to tarnish the good reputation we spent a year and a half building here. I don't like that, but there's only so much I can do. But I'm very grateful. All of you have been so kind to me. I was expecting...respect, I suppose, professionalism, I guess is closer, but not kindness."

"Well...we're kind people," David replied.

"So I'm learning. I guess I'm not helping. I'm

just dancing around the matter..." She chewed on her lower lip for a moment, reaching up and rubbing the back of her neck. "Traditionally, I'm bad with things like this." She paused again, then laughed, a mixture of anxiety and frustration. "Cait told me I should just come out with it, and I should. It's just...hard to actually *say,* you know?"

"I can understand that," he replied. "Take your time."

"Thanks." She paused once more, staring at him, and he stared back at her, waiting.

He really studied her, now that he had time, and found an interesting woman looking at him. She was tall, he saw, about as tall as he was, nearly six feet. She had a solid build, her thighs and her hips really filled out her pants, he found it hard to ignore that fact. Her skin was pale, her brown hair was down, framing her face, chin-length.

Her eyes were bright and blue. She looked...a little haunted, even now. She had a scar on her chin, and another on her forehead. He hadn't noticed them before. She didn't look mature or middle-aged, but she didn't look young, either.

Finally, she sighed. "No way to do it but to do it, I might as well just come out with it," she said. "I...want to have sex with you."

"Oh," he said. He'd...not expected her to say that, more hoped than expected. "I enthusiastically accept your offer."

She laughed. "Well...that was easy."

"Did you honestly think it wasn't going to be?" he asked.

"I mean...I don't know. I thought it might be like flipping a coin. Maybe yes, but just as likely maybe no. You're with *Cait* for God's sake. She's one of the most beautiful women I've ever seen in my life. And Ellie. And Evelyn, she is *gorgeous.* And I'm...me. A lot of men, especially younger, non-military men, are intimidated by the uniform, the lifestyle, the attitude. But I suppose I can see now why you wouldn't be intimidated."

"I wouldn't go that far," David replied. "I'm very intimidated by you. That just...doesn't stop me." He chuckled. "Vanessa told me the same thing yesterday."

"You had sex with *Vanessa?*" she asked, her eyes wide.

"I know, right?! She offered."

"Good lord, that must have been amazing. She must be eight feet tall."

"It was." He paused. "So...you're sure about this?"

"Oh yes," she replied immediately. "I'm sure. Are you?"

"Positively certainly," he said.

She smiled. "Then let's, uh, let's...do it."

"You want to wash up, first? We have a washbasin and some soap."

"Oh! Yes, excellent idea. I sweated up a fucking storm out there."

"Same."

They walked over to the washbasin he and Evelyn had set up. He liked calling it that, rather than something like a tub or bucket or whatever the fuck. Even if it was just a simple square metal container held up about three feet off the floor by a wooden table. They poured fresh melted water into it once a day and kept soap and rags nearby.

David started taking his clothes off, grateful to be out of them, honestly. Now that he was actually getting used to sleeping naked and just being naked around a lot of different women, he was finding that it was just comfortable as hell. He noticed Lara was taking her time.

"Lara," he said.

"Yeah?" she replied, still sounding anxious.

"I just want you to know that I'm not going to give you a hard time about anything. I want you to take your time. I won't get annoyed or frustrated. I want to move at a pace you're comfortable with, and if, at any moment, you decide you don't want to do this, or you aren't into what we're doing and want to change it up, or really just have anything to say, tell me directly. I'm open to communication. I want this to be good for you, and I know how awkward it can feel during the first time with someone new. I want to do whatever I can to make you feel comfortable and safe."

"Wow," she said after a few seconds, "Cait really wasn't overselling you. Thank you, I really appreciate that. It's been longer than I would care to admit since I've been sexually active. So I may be out of practice. So...thank you."

"You're welcome."

She stripped down to her bra and panties, hesitated briefly, then took off her bra and pulled her panties down and stepped out of them. He couldn't help but check her out. She was in great shape. Fit, with decently defined muscles along her arms and legs, especially her legs. She did indeed have some thick fucking thighs. And her *hips*. God*damn*! She smiled when she saw his eyes on her and turned away from him.

Looking back over her shoulder, she said, "So what do you think?"

"I think your ass is to fucking die for," he replied. "Like, *fuck,* Lara."

She laughed and faced him. Her tits were stellar. They were towards the larger end of the spectrum, almost as big as Cait's, pale and spectacularly beautiful.

"So glad I shaved yesterday," she murmured, looking down at her pussy. It had a light dusting of brown stubble.

"It *does* look nice," he murmured. "Fuck, you are *really* hot!" he added, looking her up and down. "And *tall.*"

"Oh, you like tall girls, huh?" she asked.

"Yes. Emphatically yes."

She laughed. "I guess you would, given the fact that you've been intimate with two goliath women. They don't get much taller than Vanessa." She grabbed a bar of soap and a washrag, then dunked both into the water and began to wash herself off.

David joined her. They didn't speak as they cleaned up, but he was happy to see that she was relaxing. Her movements became calmer, her stance less tense. They both washed up, dried off, and then walked over to the bed.

"I imagine you and Evelyn sleep here?" she asked as they climbed into it.

"Yep. And sometimes Cait, or Ellie, or April."

"Are *all* of you in a shared relationship? I got a clearer image, but I'm still not sure."

"Evelyn, April, Cait, and myself are all dating. Ellie and Ashley have sex with us sometimes. And Jennifer and I have slept together a few times, Vanessa and I once."

"You are quite popular," she murmured.

"Apparently," he replied. "If you don't mind my

asking, and not that I am at all complaining, obviously, but...why are you into me?" he asked as they settled in the middle of the bed. They laid down facing each other in the moonlight.

"Well...you made a *very* strong first impression on me," she admitted.

"Oh yeah?"

"Yes. The first time I saw you, well...let's just say that I've been more than a little sexually frustrated lately. And when I saw you...you're *very* attractive to me. Something about your eyes, and your chin, and your hair...I don't know. You just...you hit my buttons. So I was already hot and bothered, and then you yelled at Stern." She laughed.

"Don't take that the wrong way. The tough guy thing...I've had enough of 'tough guys' to last me three dozen lifetimes. But no one stands up to Stern, not really, and you did. And you didn't do it to prove yourself, to impress the women around you, or for any other reason than you were trying to help people. I could tell. And that just..." she exhaled sharply. "That made me *very* wet. Very horny. I've been thinking about you ever since then. So...yeah, that's why," she replied.

"Uh, okay, interesting," he said. "So...are you good to go raw?"

"Yes," she said. "And you don't have to pull out. I'm infertile. Like, I know I am. I had tests done and everything. So...yeah, we can do everything."

"That is *really* good to hear, because I want to do *everything* with you," he said.

She grinned at him, and then she leaned in and kissed him. It was like getting struck by lightning. He could feel the pulse of raw, desperate desire shoot through him as her lips met his. They were luscious and full and hot.

He let her lead as she slowly began to make out with him, pulling back ever so slightly every few seconds, as though savoring each kiss, then resuming. He liked it. He laid his hand across one of her breasts, and groaned at how perfect it felt there. It was just big enough to fit in his grasp, and her skin was hot and soft and smooth.

Lara pressed herself up against him and deepened the kiss after a few moments. She pushed him onto his back and got half up on him, reaching down and wrapping her fingers around his rigid cock. He grabbed her ass as she shoved her tongue into his mouth.

She really did have a fantastically thick ass. He twisted his tongue with hers, tasting her, enjoying her, losing himself in her. They kept going until he reversed it, pushing her onto her back and then slipping his hand in between her thick thighs. She parted them for him.

"Oh, *David...*" she moaned as he began to massage her clit.

He grinned into the kiss. "So you like that," he murmured.

"Of course, *oh!*" she moaned, then closed her eyes and began to lose herself in the pleasure. He kept kissing her and fingering her, and before long he slipped lower and began to lick one of her breasts, around her nipple several times, and then across it.

She cried out each time. He slipped a finger inside of her and began to fuck her with it, then started to suck on her nipple. She moaned his name several times as he pleasured her, though he noticed she was being much more controlled and quiet than...

Well, practically every other woman he'd taken

to this bed.

She came barely thirty seconds later, and even then she was remarkably quiet. She let out a loud moan, but that was the extent of it. No yelling or crying out. She had a lot of self control. Even still, she jerked and twitched and spasmed as he sucked on her tits and fingered her throughout the orgasm. Her powerful, broad hips heaved and her thighs clenched and released several times, and her hands tore at the blankets beneath her as she squirted.

And then she was finished, and panting, and her eyes opened.

"Fuck me," she said, staring straight up. Then she twisted to look at him. "Make love to me right now, David. Please."

"Okay," he replied, and got on top of her, settling in between her thick, pale thighs.

She gripped his cock and helped him into her immediately, and oh holy fucking shit the perfect, slick, hot pleasure of her pussy as she took him into her. She was *tight* and incredibly wet. She moaned loudly, grabbing his back as he worked his way into her.

"You're big," she moaned. "Cait said...you were big...fuck...oh yeah..."

He kissed her and she responded immediately, kissing him back hard, slipping a hand up over the back of his head. As he began making love to her, sliding smoothly in and out of her pussy, he felt a surprisingly intense connection with her, a powerful intimacy that normally wasn't present during first time sex.

He loved it, and could feel her responding to it as well. She moaned and kissed him with an almost desperate passion. Soon, she had wrapped her legs around him, running her hands up and down his back, holding him against her.

She moaned his name again and again, as he did hers.

They made love in the moonlit dimness of his bedroom, and in that moment, it felt like it was just the two of them, locked together in lust and bliss and intimacy and deep sexual gratification.

"Oh David...I'm going to come again," she panted.

"Me too," he moaned. "You feel *amazing,* Lara."

"Let's come together. I want to come together."

"Yes," he groaned, and started going faster.

Now she was panting and moaning loudly, getting noisier, and the pleasure seemed to double, triple, beginning to overwhelm him. Fucking her bare, raw vagina was blindingly blissful, filling him with a pure rapturous ecstasy that only sex seemed to be able to bring. She pushed against him with her big hips, squeezing him with her legs, holding him against her with her hands, kissing him deeply. He felt locked with her in shared bliss.

And then she began to come. She moaned loudly into the kiss, staring into his eyes, and he felt her vaginal muscles clench and flutter, and another hot spray of sex juices begin to escape her. That was it, he could hold on no longer.

David began to come inside of her. He started to release his seed into her, and he joined her in moaning loudly, losing himself completely within her. They came together, and it felt like a perfect moment in a cold, painful world. They had each other, and this shared connection, and in that moment nothing else mattered.

They rode that high together for several minutes

after coming down from the orgasm, laying together, the sweat cooling on their bodies.

"Wow," Lara said finally.

He chuckled. "Yeah."

"That was..."

"Amazing."

"Uh-huh."

They laid there for a bit longer. "Maybe we should get back downstairs."

"I guess so...where will I sleep tonight?" she murmured.

"You can sleep here, in this bed, if you'd like."

"Yeah, I'd like that. It's been *so* long since I've shared a bed with someone."

They laid together for another moment, then David's need to figure out what it was that Cait had to tell him overrode his comfort in laying there with Lara, and he got up. They took a moment to wash themselves, then dressed, and began to head back downstairs. He took Lara's hand, and she smiled, laced their fingers, and laid her head on his shoulder.

It was a simple but deeply satisfying gesture. They walked back down to the ground floor, and found everyone still hanging around, drinking or chatting or just relaxing.

He saw Cait hanging out with Ellie and Jennifer on a couch in the corner. They all smiled at him as he and Lara walked over.

"You two look satisfied," Ellie said.

"Yes. It was a...*very* satisfying experience," Lara replied, a little awkwardly.

David nodded in agreement, then fixed his gaze on Cait, who stared back at him a little sheepishly. She got to her feet. "You've been very patient with me, honey," she said, "and I'm sorry for having to keep you in the dark about this. You have to understand that this was very much a surprise to me." She reached out and took his hand.

"I understand. Or I'm trying to...so what is it, Cait? What's happened?" he asked.

Looking into his eyes, she said, "I'm pregnant with your child, David."

ABOUT ME

I am Misty Vixen (not my real name obviously), and I imagine that if you're reading this, you want to know a bit more about me.

In the beginning (late 2014), I was an erotica author. I wrote about sex, specifically about human men banging hot inhuman women. Monster girls, alien ladies, paranormal babes. It was a lot of fun, but as the years went on, I realized that I was actually striving to be a harem author. This didn't truly occur to me until late 2019-early 2020. Once the realization fully hit, I began doing research on what it meant to be a harem author. I'm kind of a slow learner, so it's taken me a bit to figure it all out.

That being said, I'm now a harem author!

Just about everything I write nowadays is harem fiction: one man in loving, romantic, highly sexual relationships with several women.

I'd say beyond writing harems, I tend to have themes that I always explore in my fiction, and they encompass things like trust, communication, respect, honesty, dealing with emotional problems in a mature way…basically I like writing about functional and healthy relationships. Not every relationship is perfect, but I don't really do drama unless the story actually calls for it. In total honesty, I hate drama. I hate people lying to each other and I hate needless rom-com bullshit plots that could have been solved by two characters have a goddamned two minute conversation.

Check out my website
www.mistyvixen.com

Here, you can find some free fiction, a monthly newsletter, alternate versions of my cover art where the ladies are naked, and more!

Check out my twitter
www.twitter.com/Misty_Vixen

I update fairly regularly and I respond to pretty much everyone, so feel free to say something!

Finally, if you want to talk to me directly, you can send me an e-mail at my address:
mistyvixen@outlook.com

Thank you for reading my work! I hope you enjoyed reading it as much as I enjoyed writing it!

-Misty

Made in the USA
Monee, IL
12 January 2024